PRAISE FOR IAN STANSEL

"Ian Stansel's Midwest is not unlike Sherwood Anderson's, a place inhabited intimately and impressively, with an especially appealing sweep of time. One comes away from this book feeling as if she'd been handed a core sample of the American experience. I highly recommend."
Antonya Nelson

"Ian Stansel's *Everybody's Irish* is remarkable in every way. The stories pulse with life, shine with insight and revelation, and lodge in your memory. By turns surprising, heart-rending, and darkly, refreshingly funny, the collection illustrates again and again not just what short stories can do, but what they must do."
Bret Anthony Johnston, author of *Corpus Christi*

"These are stories of profound heart and deeply resonant humanity. I'm giddy to finally have all of Ian Stansel's gorgeously crafted and emotionally affecting stories bound together in one volume that I can read and reread. *Everybody's Irish* is my most-anticipated-book-of-the-year— and I'd wager that's true for anyone who's read even a single story by him."
Thisbe Nissen, author of *The Good People of New York* and *Osprey Island*

"Ian Stansel's smart, accomplished stories crackle with awareness and pulse with quiet compassion."
Megan Mayhew Bergman, author of *Birds of a Lesser Paradise*

"The nine elegant and haunting tales in *Everybody's Irish* mark the debut of a wonderfully talented writer."
Jennifer Vanderbes, author of *Easter Island* and *Strangers at the Feast*

EVERYBODY'S IRISH

Stories

Ian Stansel

FIVECHAPTERS
BOOKS

*All rights reserved. Published in the United States by
FiveChapters*

www.fivechapters.com
www.ianstansel.com

Publication Acknowledgments

"Dukes and Duchesses of Park Ridge": Ploughshares
"A Dry Season": Ecotone;
New Stories from the Midwest 2012
"The Ridiculous Future": The Journal
"Domestique": Five Chapters
"The Tall Lake Grasses": Sycamore Review
"All We Have": Antioch Review
"Everybody's Irish": Memorious
"Traveling Light": Cincinnati Review

Book interior design by Maya Sariahmed

Manufactured in the United States of America
Published August 2013
First printing

For Sarah

Contents

Dukes and Duchesses of Park Ridge

We constructed a sign and planted it in the park in the center of town. *Future Site of the First National Bank of the Grand Duchy of New Brunswick.* As best as anyone could remember, Stephen came up with the idea itself. Lisa added "New Brunswick." Donna contributed "Grand Duchy." She'd read it in the encyclopedia and everyone loved the term. We cut the wood in Matt's parents' garage. The sign was four-by-five feet and had a picture of the supposed building on it: a six-story glass-and-steel cube rising from the unsuspecting soil of the town. Joel painted it. An artist's rendering of an artist's rendering. Joel was back from art school in Rhode Island. We were all visiting that summer, back for a few months from school, where we hid out from work and the draft in dorm rooms and classrooms and pool halls, trying to figure out how to live lives in the middle of all that America. It was 1967 and for most of us it was the last time we'd be back in this way, before committing ourselves to other places, falling in love with other people. We were still each other's family and lovers then, still focused fully on waking each other up.

There was a hint of cool in the dark and silent night. We

did it in shifts. Three arrived with post-hole diggers, then a few minutes later others came through with the sign in the back of Swope's truck, the '56 Chevy—half-busted and rusted-out after a dozen Midwestern winters—that he'd bought off a farmer in Iowa. They set the sign, filled the holes, packed it in and headed out. Clockwork. A few hours later in the purple and orange of the early morning twilight, Carrie was there in the middle of town, across from the park, to take pictures of all the people checking it out. She had been the photo editor of the yearbook at South. (Most of us had gone to South, but after high school we lost some and gained others from elsewhere: East, Glenview, Niles, even a few from Chicago proper.) She had a great big Nikon and her folks wouldn't tear up her closet darkroom in the basement for a few more years. She snapped away from behind the brick corner of Moheiser's department store as the morning walkers came by and saw.

The older folks, early risers that they are, arrived first. They gathered and pointed, shook their heads, and gestured toward it and each other. Carrie got one shot of a man tapping the sign with his cane, his face in a cartoonish grimace. This became a favorite of ours. We liked them, these elders of ours. They wouldn't stand for this business, not in their park. Moms and babies came next, growing the crowd. The mothers exchanged words with their older counterparts, but eventually migrated towards one another, strollers arranged in a semi-circle around one end of the sign. And the suited men of our town watched their wives and children and elders from the platform, and then from the windows of their trains, accelerating eastbound into the city.

As the morning grew brighter and more people came, Swope joined Carrie and the two of them infiltrated the crowd. They came round and Swope took Carrie's hand. "Just a couple a sweethearts on a nice morning walk," he said.

They had known each other for years now, since middle

school, but had never, as far as either of them could remember, really talked. They were not, as Carrie would have phrased it, each other's *primaries*. On our group trips to the movies or miniature golf, and later to forest preserves to drink beers and smoke cigarettes pilfered from our parents' stashes, Carrie and Swope spoke in passing, understanding each others' general references, but never having any of their own. Yes, they would have called each other "friend" to an outsider, but it would have been with an imperceptible hesitation. A momentary pause to acknowledge the inadequacies of our all too general categories.

The rest of us decided they should witness the scene and report back. They were two of the least incendiary looking of us, both still holding onto their Midwestern good looks and politeness of dress. Carrie had her dark hair back in a ponytail. Swope even wore the letterman jacket he got while playing tailback for South.

"What is *this*?" Carrie said to Swope, loud enough for the folks around them to hear.

"Sweetie," an older woman said, "that's what we're all trying to figure out here."

Soon the cops came by. The two of them got out of their patrol, set cups of coffee on the roof, and surveyed the commotion before stepping forward. It didn't take long—a few muffled announcements and questions and requests through the car's two-way—to come to the conclusion that it was a hoax. Through the speaker a woman's voice: "Mayor says take it down."

"Sure he doesn't want to come down and have a look?"

The woman crackled through the speaker: "You're welcome to head over to his house and ask him, but I'm warning you he hasn't had his coffee yet."

"Alright," the officer said, resigned.

Carrie stepped across the street and got shots of the two

cops—both of them thick men, bellies hanging over their belts—as they pushed and pulled the sign, loosening the dirt around the posts. "We packed it in pretty good," Swope whispered to Carrie, his mouth close to her ear. She turned slightly, the camera still in front of her face, and smiled.

One of the cops stopped and looked up at Carrie. "You know anything about this?" The crowd turned toward her.

"No, sir."

"You got that camera, though, huh."

"I just happen to," Carrie said. "Lucky break, too, with all this craziness."

The sign came down in just a few minutes. In total, it took us ten hours to make; it stayed up for just about five. It was big enough that the cops had to carry it, awkwardly, to City Hall, where they deposited it in the back parking lot, leaning against the fence. Carrie developed the pictures and sold one for fifteen bucks to the *Herald*. It was on the cover of the afternoon edition that very day. That evening we excitedly met up at the diner.

The host grunted and without asking how many we'd be, took a stack of menus and walked to the back booth of the restaurant. This was where he always sat us. Away from the general population. The back booth was enclosed on three sides—a cubby for birthday parties and other large gatherings. And for us, whose mere presence seemed to affront the host to such a degree that he would seat even just two or three of us there, where we'd be out of sight, leaving larger parties to awkwardly push together the round tables of the main dining room.

Carrie had made sure to get one shot of the Grand Duchy sign by itself, without the commotion around it, the details of the work clear. This one she handed to Joel. "For your portfolio," she said. She fanned the rest of the pictures across the table.

"I love this," Lisa said, picking up a shot of a tall young mother leaning down to a woman three times her age. Donna, Matt, Stephen, Georgia, Swope, Kurt and all of us traded the photos, laughed and remembered the prior night.

—

Sometimes we made love to one another. Not a lot, but sometimes. Despite what the world would say, neither the sex nor the drugs were not that prevalent. Really we were a bunch of kids from the suburbs, in so many ways just like those who came before and those who would follow, a thousand questions filling our heads for any one inkling of an answer. But sometimes. Sometimes we took that step, smashing ourselves against each other in our dorms or the backs of station wagons.

Swope was at the diner a few nights later when Carrie came in. He lit a cigarette and waved her over, asked her what she was up to.

"Thought I'd grab some pie maybe, some coffee."

"Join me."

Swope was back from the University of Iowa. A physics major at that moment, but it would change the next semester to mathematics, and then again to botany, and then near the end of his second year he would finally settle, like so many young men at the time, on political science.

"The problem," he said to Carrie as her slice of blueberry was set in front of her, "is that I want to do everything. You choose one thing and that means you're giving up on the rest. That's the problem with careers."

"I guess it's a matter of finding what you can do the most in."

"But the thing you have the most ability in might not be the thing that you want to do the most."

"Accomplishment isn't only a matter of ability, though. It's also about what you enjoy. If you don't want to do the thing, then you probably won't. Or not well. Or not for long, anyway."

Swope thought about this for a moment. Carrie ate a forkful of her pie without taking her eyes off Swope and his thinking.

"You're smart," Swope said finally.

"Maybe," Carrie said. "We'll have to see how it all plays out. Right now I'm just talking."

Carrie had meant to spend the summer down in Champaign, until a mix-up at the housing office left her dorm-less. So instead of skulking the library and the quad, she was haunting the diner and the town's shops. Most of her friends from school were home for the summer anyway, but she'd been looking forward to the quiet, to walking around for a couple months, to reading books and catching the same movie over and over at the Art Theater.

"And you're sure," Swope said, "that you dig what you're doing enough."

Carrie thought about his phrasing and wondered if Swope knew what it was she studied. "I have no idea," she said. "It's working so far."

She scooped some of the last of the pie and gestured it towards him. He leaned forward and wrapped his mouth around the morsel, pulled back and left the fork shining clean.

"You're lucky," he said. "If the psychology ends up being a drag, you've got photography."

Carrie looked at him with new intensity, leaning forward, squinting her eyes.

"What's up?" Swope said.

"E-N," she said slowly, without changing her expression, "T-J. That's my best guess for you. Your personality type."

"Is that good?"

"Oh, it's not good or bad," she said leaning back, relaxing

her brow. "There's no judgment, man. It's just interesting is all. It's also probably totally unethical of me as a future psychologist to throw out guesses like that. Oh, well."

"So, what, those letters stand for different things about me?"

"Extrovertion, Intuition, Thinking, Judging. Of course, you'd have to take a real test to find out for sure. We had to take it, like, right off the bat. First week of class. Our teacher's big into Jung, you know?"

"So, what'd you get?"

"E-N-F-P. Extrovertion, Intuition, Feeling, Percieving."

"Yours sounds better than mine. Mine sounds like I judge people. Mine sounds like I'm a dick."

"That's not what it means. Seriously. And, anyway, I'm probably totally wrong. One of these days we'll go to the library and get a real test and have you take it."

A half hour later, when they got to it, the house was cool and dark. Swope's parents were out to dinner. It had a smell, cigarettes and ripe fruit, that Swope didn't notice—he hadn't been gone long enough yet—and that reminded Carrie that she did not know this boy Swope well at all. But the mystery was appealing. To find that there was any mystery left in Park Ridge, where she'd spent her entire life, where she had learned to walk and think and feel, was appealing. There was a touch of light coming through the picture window and she could see just the muzzy outline of his back and head. Then he turned and his pale face seemed to grab all of that light and glow hazily, without definition, like a face only half-imagined. They ascended the stairs and Swope led Carrie into his young-boy bedroom. He turned on a dim bedside lamp and put on a record, something that Carrie didn't recognize, something folky and beautiful, with strings accompanying a mellow guitar and imploring voice. Swope came to where Carrie stood, still near the door, and took both her hands in his.

"Two sweethearts on a walk," she said.

—

Soon we were planning a new stunt. The sign was not the first one we'd pulled and with more and more of us becoming emboldened by university atmospheres we were quicker to get over small victories, quicker to bore. We were soon back at Matt's parents' garage to construct a casket for the beach. It was full size and black. We pooled our money for the hardware. The inside we lined with plastic sheeting so that it would be waterproof.

That weekend, we loaded the thing into the back of Swope's truck (joking that we'd never get anything done if he hadn't bought the jalopy) and caravanned to Glencoe. We were dressed in our (or our parents') most somber black. Our hair was pulled back neatly. The beach was crowded, as we all knew it would be. The sun high and unveiled. The water lapping at the feet of shrieking children. We walked, pallbearers and mourners, the casket hoisted shoulder high, to an open patch of sand. It was as if even the water quieted. The entire population of the beach looked at us, confused, alarmed, repulsed. We set the coffin down and the lid squeaked beautifully as it was opened, as if we'd planned it somehow, a dramatic horror movie squeak. A vampire waking. Some mothers took hold of their kids. Men made a show of gesturing toward us. But mostly they just stared, like children who'd been moved in their sleep and who now, half-awake, were trying to understand their new surroundings.

Matt, being the one who completed most of the construction of the box, took charge and was the first to reach his hand in and grab an Old Style. As soon as he pulled it open we each grabbed one out of the sloshing ice water, loosened our ties and rolled our pant legs, letting the foam of the beer run down our chins. Getting down to the business of living is how we thought of it. Our fellow beach-goers didn't agree. A woman said, "Shame on you." Others said, "Go home, hippies." We were still working on our first beers, still with most of our toes dry, when a group of men began to organize. We tried to seem as if we weren't watching and getting nervous.

Of course, we also, in many ways, wanted the attention, wanted the confrontation. It was a reaction that we strove to get with almost everything we did, whether from one another or strangers. We spent our days smiling and laughing (often more broadly, more loudly than would be natural, proving we could), sitting on the grass outside the library and reading books and talking for hours in the back booth of the diner. We waved and said good morning and afternoon and evening to everyone, especially those we knew would not say anything back—the stuffy businessmen heading to and from the train, old ladies stopping in at Fannie May Candies for their weekly fix of caramels and mint meltaways. We did not think we were unique. We didn't think we were doing anything that wasn't being done elsewhere. Every town, we figured, had its group of merry pranksters. We counted on it. That was the thing— there had to be others, or what chance did any of us have?

The men, pale and hairy and barrel-chested, approached. "Okay," one of them said, his voice nasally and Chicago. "You've had your laughs, now it's time to get this thing gone."

"We haven't even gotten our feet wet," Matt said.

"And you aren't gonna."

Swope picked up a couple cans of Old Style and held them out. "Why don't you guys join us?"

The man closest to him slapped the cans out of Swope's hand. One splashed back into the casket water. The other landed with a *pfftt* in the sand. Carrie raised her hands and nervously touched the tips of her fingers to her mouth. She felt at that moment that she might be in love with Swope.

The men paid no attention to the girls, only focused on the boys, who had no intention of fighting. We didn't fight. That was part of the point. There were confrontations, and we wouldn't fight. There was war, and we would not fight.

Plus, of course, we stood no chance against these men. Even the strongest of us, Swope or Matt, wouldn't have lasted more than a minute with these dads with their dad-strength. It was one of the few times in life when we were happy to see the cops. A patrol car pulled up to the entrance of the beach and a voice from a speaker said, "Alright, stand down, gentlemen."

—

That night Carrie and Swope lay in his bed, a breeze coming through the open window, a sheet covering their thin bodies. "I thought that guy was gonna pop you one," she said.

"Shit, me too," Swope said. "I bet everyone did. I bet the only one who didn't think he was gonna pop me one was him."

"You don't think he would have?"

"He might have, but I'm saying that that guy was probably doing everything to avoid thinking directly about popping me one. I bet he wouldn't have known he was going to do it until he was already doing it. I don't think most people can seriously think about doing something like that and then go through with it. I was on vacation with my folks a bunch of years ago and we were at this diner, and there was this couple at a table and everything was fine until the lady starts raising her voice. Raising her voice in a way that says she's trying not to, you know? And the guy was obviously getting uncomfortable being yelled at in public, and he was trying to get her to calm down. They left finally and we finished our dinner, but they were still in the parking lot when we got out of there. And they were really going at it now, screaming right in each other's faces. I don't have a clue what it was about, but I remember one thing, that at some point while we were crossing to our car the woman said, 'What are you going to do, hit me?' My mom put her hand on my back and hurried me up and my dad slowed down and looked back. We got in the car and just kept on going with our vacation, but I remembered that question, 'What are you going to do, hit me?' The way I figure it, she was making the guy consider it, hitting her. And then there was almost no chance of it actually happening. Violence happens when you don't think."

Swope did not know where these ideas came from. He hadn't considered them before. He had not thought of that couple in the parking lot in years. And then he was suddenly in silent awe of what a brain can do, and he understood why Carrie would want to study it.

"Maybe that's what we need for this war," Carrie said. "Someone sitting in all those planes saying to the pilot, 'What are you going to do, bomb that town?' 'What are you going to do, kill all those people?' Make them think about it."

"Yeah, and even higher up, standing next to the generals, 'Hey, what are you going to do, give that order? Don't you know that innocent people will die?' It would be like a replacement conscience for the one they all lose during training."

Swope got up and walked naked to the window, where his cigarettes were sitting on the sill. He sat on the floor and lit one, trying to direct the stream of smoke out into the humid night.

"How come we never really talked before, all those years?" Carrie asked.

"You were too pretty. I was intimidated."

"Horseshit."

Swope smiled and took a drag off his cigarette. He remained silent on the subject. But Carrie knew the answer.

Sometime in the past year, in a class or in his dorm or dining hall, or maybe even the morning he left Park Ridge, huddled in the back of his parents' wagon, his few possessions boxed up and stacked in the very back, on his way to Iowa—maybe during those few hours, something happened. The alarm bell went off and Swope woke up. He was a different person now— no longer a sleepy-headed kid, not quite a man yet, but a person taking his first steps towards a real and honest existence. The kid she knew before was gone, and though that kid was kind and honest and intelligent—as far as she ever knew—this person sitting on the floor, dragging on a smoke, naked as the day, had the potential for the extraordinary. Carrie felt that she herself was going through the same experience, but that did not stop her from admiring him for his own journey.

—

It was planned as a gathering to garner national attention. Swope heard about it from a friend from school. In the diner he explained to the rest of us that it would be thousands of people swarming into this one small town, just on the Illinois side of the Mississippi. The town had elected a haircut hippie as mayor the year before (he was fighting to keep large agribusiness out of the town and the farmers had voted him in overwhelmingly—hippie or not) and he made sure all the permits were signed and legitimate. The point was to bring the movement to Everytown. It could be that town, or this one, or the one you call home, was what we'd be saying.

"Some little podunk farmtown?" Joel said. "Sounds like a drag."

Carrie chimed in, "I love it. We'll be getting to where the living happens."

"Or," Swope said to Joel, "we can stick around here and play some more tricks on people. Maybe some fake vomit in the library? Whoopie cushions?"

We made our plans. It would take three cars. At this point we all knew Carrie would be riding with Swope in his truck. They were developing into a partnership that we thought made sense. But we all silently wondered what would happen in the fall when it was time for us all to once again scatter across the country in cars, buses, on trains, to our other lives. A few hundred miles was so far at that time, at that age. No one said anything, though. Most of us were without romance or sex, so it was good to see happening for some. The rest of us tried to remain focused on this latest happening. We put our energy and passion there. We gave our love to the world, abstract and pained.

We met in front of Swope's house at six o'clock on the morning of the rally. Each of us brought whatever supplies we could: cans of soda and Thermoses of water, fruit, candy bars, cold-cut and cheese sandwiches. We dumped it all out on the bed of the truck and distributed it so that everyone would have enough to get them through the day. On the highway, Carrie slid in close to Swope and they watched the houses spread out and the lawns turn to fields of corn, each stalk seeming to wake up and stretch toward the rising eastern sun.

To pass the time, Carrie had gone to the library and copied the questions to a Jungian personality test. She read the questions aloud and marked down Swope's answers. Swope felt no discomfort in the process. He found that he trusted Carrie almost completely. He answered as honestly as he could, taking a few moments to think about each question. He wanted the result to be accurate, to tell him something about himself, some understanding that he could keep and use. Carrie calculated the responses and it turned out that Swope's type was just as she had predicted. "A total coincidence," she said, but Swope knew that she had an uncommon insight into him.

The rally was apparent as soon as they neared the town. Cars lined the sides of the highway and all of the gravel roads jutting north and south. Rows of people—beautiful, smiling, young and old—walked west along the embankment. "Looks like we're hoofing it," Swope said. He pulled over and the rest of us did the same. We got out of our cars and in the distance we could hear the beginnings of organization: the muffled din of the crowd, the occasional bullhorn shout, cheers in reaction. We held hands and swung arms over shoulders joined the march. This was it, the world in miraculous flux.

The day was already turning warm. The walk down the road took nearly a half hour, but all fatigue and soreness dissipated as we arrived. The town itself was a mere four blocks of two-story buildings, the front windows displaying antique wood furniture and small appliances and older residents settling down at red-and-white checked tables. Yellow painted saw-horses kept cars off this main drag. A couple of us commented on this or that aspect of the town, but mostly we'd been driven to silence by what seemed very likely to be the culmination of our young lives. We fantasized about dropping out of our schools and moving to this tiny burg. Getting a piece of land. Tilling and farming and harvesting. Swimming in mellow, green tributaries of the Mississippi. Nights on the porch of some gorgeous little clapboard shack. Surely others would come. Surely of the thousands there on that July day we were not the only ones picturing a more permanent gathering. A lifelong happening.

Carrie squeezed Swope's hand. Swope squeezed Carrie's hand. We went to the west edge of town, where the main crowd had organized. Many had brought signs and we wondered how we had neglected to do the same. Down a side street was a cordoned off area where men in suits held microphones in front of bulky cameras. We found a circle of space within the crowd. A small stage had been erected on the lawn of the town's one-room library. A man stood center holding the bullhorn we'd heard back down the road. He spoke—muffled but passionate. "The people of this town," he said, "and a thousand others like it know the true cost of our actions in Vietnam far better than those men in Washington ever could." We cheered in agreement. He continued. "Those in Washington are our employees—we hired them and we pay their salaries, and it's about time they to do as they're told and end this war." We cheered louder, our faces turning red with excitement.

The rally lasted all day. People laughed and passed joints. Carrie and Swope snuck off and found an empty curb to sit and eat their lunch. Carrie removed the slices of ham from her ham and cheese and said, "I decided to not eat meat anymore." Swope took the meat from his own sandwich and said, "Me too, then." Carrie piled the meat onto a flattened paper bag and Swope held it out in offering to a trio of laughing teens, who took it gratefully. In the heat of the mid-afternoon, the local fire department got out the hoses and sprayed easy streams of water into the air far above us and it came down in a cooling rain. We cheered even louder than we had for any of the speakers.

Until dusk we listened to men and women take their turns on the stage. We talked to the town's citizens. At eight o'clock the rally ended and we felt that we'd been successful, that in some way we'd made a difference with our hours. People would discuss this—people who weren't there would talk about it and know that even here in this small town in Illinois people were standing up and demanding a change from the policies of war and destruction.

In the confusion of the exodus, Swope and Carrie were

separated from the rest of us. We stood on tippy-toes trying to catch sight of them over the rest of the eastward moving throng. They were lost among the thousands. We were sure that they'd meet us at the car. After thirty minutes at the car, we were sure they'd meet us back at the diner.

—

They had decided to let the crowd go first. Neither was in a great hurry to leave. They wanted to keep the feeling for a little while longer, to ease out of the day slowly. The town emptied out, quieted. The shadows of street-side trees lengthened. It was dark by the time they got to the truck, now alone on the side of miles and miles of highway. They U-turned and Swope pulled a joint from between the seat cushions. Carrie lit it and took a deep, grateful drag, and they passed it back and forth. The night was almost black there in the country. Stars appeared one by one, first the brightest of them and then the others, farther and more modestly lit. "They say there are like a hundred billion neurons in the human brain," Carrie said. "But really, I don't think we have a fucking clue how it works." The road became illuminated in blue and red. A quick siren shouted. Swope stubbed out the roach of the joint and then popped it into his mouth and swallowed. He opened his window and pulled to the side of the road. Carrie opened the window on her side. Swope lit a cigarette. After a minute, two police officers approached on either side of the truck.

"License," the first one said to Swope. Swope handed it over. "You two heading home?"

"Yeah."

"Where you coming from?"

"We're just driving," Swope said.

"Well, you have to be coming from somewhere. There

has to be a start point. You two must have been at that party a ways back earlier."

"We, uh—"

The cop on Carrie's side interrupted. "How about you," he said to Carrie. "Let's get some ID." He looked at Carrie's license, then he said, "I have to tell you, I am smelling something coming from inside this truck."

Swope held up his cigarette. "Want one?"

"I don't think that's it," the one on Swope's side said. "You see that turn-off up ahead?" he asked, pointing up the road. "We're going to need you to pull up there. We'll be right behind." He kept Swope's license and took a step towards their patrol car. Then he stopped and said, "And don't try and gun it on outta here. You're not making it far in this thing." He rapped a knuckle against the truck's side.

"It's fine," Swope said to Carrie as they slowly pulled forward. "That's all I had in here. Do you have anything?"

"No."

"Okay, then, it's fine."

The narrow turn-off was gravel and the stones knocked loudly against the undercarriage of the truck. Swope slowed, but the cop tapped on his horn. Swope pulled further down the road, but again the cop honked. They were several hundred yards from the highway by the time they were allowed to stay put and cut the engine.

Again the cops came up to the truck. They each held flashlights. "All right, both of you out." They did so. "Now, if we were to look through this truck, are we going to find anything that you think we as police officers might disapprove of?"

"No, sir."

"What do you think, ma'am?" the other one said to Carrie.

"No, sir."

"Did you indulge in any illegal substances back there at

your little party?"

"No, sir," Carrie said. "We just want to get home."

"I'm sure that's true," the one on Carrie's side said, looking at his partner. He waited a beat and then handed Carrie her license. "I guess you should be on your way, then." The other cop gave Swope his ID. "Have a peaceful night," he said. Swope and Carrie watched the cops walk to their car and four-point-turn back toward the highway. The rattling car receded into the distance.

Swope laughed a quick breath. "Well, shit."

"Let's go," Carrie said.

They were halfway turned around, perpendicular to the road, when another car approached quickly. Swope looked to his left at the oncoming lights. "Hang on, hang on," he said. The car skidded to a stop. Four men emerged and rushed the truck. "Whoa, whoa," Swope began. Two went to the far side and opened the door. Carrie screamed as they pulled her from the cab. Swope reached toward Carrie, but the other two opened his door and dragged him out onto the gravel. Swope felt the first fist as if it came from inside his head, something trying to punch its way out. His eyes swam. The lights of the other car multiplied in his vision. Another fist, and then a kick in the stomach. He heard nothing except the scrape of shoes on the ground. The lights of the car felt so bright that it was a relief when legs would pass in front of them and momentarily shadow him. He weakly threw gravel into the air. More kicking.

A hand held Carrie's head to the ground. Her face pressed into the dirt and stones. She struggled but another hand yanked her arm behind her back. A leg pushed into her lower back. She breathed in short gasps. Beneath the car, she could see the other side. It was all black silhouetted forms. Dust floating in shafts of lights. A mound moving in convulsive jerks and starts. Then the weight on top of her eased and she turned to her side and punched, making contact with what she thought might be a neck. She was halfway up when hands pushed her and she stumbled down hard toward the front of the truck.

Swope recognized vague sounds of speech, words that in the moment he could not put meaning to, and then the kicking stopped. Legs became lost behind the light. Tires flung dust and rocks into him and he kept his hands over his face. The lights of the men's car shrank as it moved backwards, away. Swope tasted blood and he tasted dirt. Breathing was difficult, but he felt no pain yet. Leaning into the side of the truck, he managed his way to his feet. The hum of the engine against his body. In the headlight stream of the truck, Carrie lay on the ground. He said her name. He said her name again.

—

Our phones rang the next morning. We found out one by one. No details, just the fact of the matter. When we couldn't get through to Swope on the phone we drove to his parents' only to find the house empty. We gathered in twos and threes in bedrooms, waiting to hear something, anything. We cried. We accepted the condolences of our parents and saw their own tears and tried to answer questions about the night before as best we could. We felt like children. We thought over and over that we should have waited for them, or that they should not have stayed behind. We should have remained together. None of us said these things. Someone spoke to someone who said, "Trauma to the head."

Swope was in a bed at Cook County General after having gotten initial treatment in Rockford. He'd suffered a fractured cheek bone, three broken ribs, and purple-black bruises covered his torso and face. The white of his right eye was red. We went to see him, but most of the time he was asleep, or he told his parents to tell us he was asleep. It took a while, but we came to understand, in bits and pieces, some of what had happened. He spoke drowsily of the night.

The police, he said, and then another car, four men. She had held his hand as the crowd left and the town grew quiet. Blood poured from her temple. She looked as though she was smiling. She had wanted to spend the summer in Champaign, reading books. He lifted her into the cab of his truck. The truck wanted to go into the ditches lining the narrow road. Local police or state troopers, he didn't know. He used his shirt on her head, but the sleeve kept falling into her face. She had gotten his type right off the bat, the genius. He spotted the lights of a gas station and almost hit a dumpster on his way in. The kid behind the counter was spooked by the blood. The ambulance took forever. No, he didn't see their faces. The lights came from behind them, he said. Her eyes were open, he said. A hundred billion neurons, he said.

—

Swope stayed in his house the last four weeks of summer. We didn't see him. He came out only to speak with the police for initial statements, and then again when they called and told him that they'd taken in suspects. In the station, he asked an officer if these were the men, and the officer said that that was what a court was for. Swope asked him again and the officer said quietly, "Yes, we believe so." He told Swope that he would most likely be asked to testify. The two police officers who pulled Swope and Carrie over were investigated, but not charged with any crime. Word was, though, that town pressure forced them to be transferred to departments downstate. The people of the town didn't care what an investigation did or didn't turn up.

Joel flew out of O'Hare and landed in Providence at the

same time Georgia was flying clear across to Los Angeles. Matt drove himself to Tallahassee with the windows down. Most of us embarked on less dramatic trips: Stephen to Evansville; Lisa to St. Louis; Kurt to Lincoln. Others to Carbondale, DeKalb, Muncie, and just down the road to Bloomington-Normal. Swope insisted on taking a bus back to Iowa City. He asked his father to sell the truck. Through that fall semester, Swope went to classes, was friendly to a new dorm mate, tried to pay attention to the changing weather, and found a quiet corner of the library where he worked and napped.

The trial of the four men coincided with the beginning of winter break, and so in the second week of December Swope was back in Park Ridge. The town donned its holiday attire: garlands on the light posts, wreathes in the windows. The tall pine in the park, the one that would have been squashed by our fictitious bank, that First National of the Grand Duchy of New Brunswick, was decorated with lights and ornaments made by kids at the elementary school. A dusting of snow over it all.

That night we met at the diner. We hugged and kept from crying by talking of holiday trivialities. We drank coffee and smoked cigarettes. We talked about our classes, about boys and girls the others did not know, would probably never know. We talked about what was happening on our campuses: the protests, the collisions with cops and administrators, the pranks we were pulling, the songs we were hearing and singing. We did not mention Carrie. We did not say her name because Swope did not say her name.

The next day Swope would go into a courthouse and face four men who hated us enough to attack. Or perhaps it was just for sport, a lark. Their stories would differ and change, these four men who gave us our first casualty of the war.

We piled into cars and drove west to stand bundled outside that courthouse. To be there as Swope walked with his father up the stairs and went out of sight behind the heavy wood doors. To be there when he came out. And when we arrived we were surprised to find a scene not unlike that day when we all caravanned to stand up against the violence so many thousands of miles away. But this time the crowd was quiet. We took up the lawn of the courthouse. Police put up yellow barriers to give us our space. The trial lasted just three days, and for each of those days the crowd grew, spilling out onto the street. When the guilty verdicts were announced we didn't cheer. But we were there, wide awake, our arms embracing one another, our chests swollen from just looking around, from knowing that we'd been right all along, that there were more of us, thousands of us, maybe millions.

Introduction by the Author

Publishers have asked for introductory words before and I've always declined, but it seems that with age I am going soft. So here we are. I find myself unconvinced that these pages will illuminate the novel or its characters of Hal and Tasha in any way (in fact, I rather doubt it), but since I did agree to provide something to accompany the new edition you hold in your hands I might as well take this opportunity to address one glaring absence from my storytelling career.

But first: at a recent gathering, I overheard a young graduate student assert that, "Every good rock star wants to be a writer, and every bad writer wishes he was a rock star." It was a fundraising event for a well-respected and impoverished literary review, and I'd been invited (and paid) to speak on the "writing life," a topic I have been reluctant to discuss before, as the phrase holds little meaning for me. The evening was pleasant and largely forgettable, except for the young man's remark, which was just the sort of self-congratulatory *bon mot* that I'd love to untangle from my synaptic bramble (though Lord knows I've uttered a bounty of them myself), but which will stick like a nasty burr in a brain such as mine. It forced me to consider all variety of unpleasantries like *aspiration* and *ability*, when all I wanted to do was retrieve a promised post-talk glass of something red. Well. No going back. While I've had what most people would rightly call a successful time of writing, as evidenced by the book you hold in your hands and others (I've been assured) heading to reprints (depending on the receipts from this one, alas), and I would never denigrate the literary community that has provided me with the means to live a comfortable and well-fed life, the fact is that the only thing I've ever wanted to be is a painter.

Now the novel. Upon its release there was a fair amount of discussion of what was fiction and what was fact. I have remained silent on the subject for two reasons: one, what has happened in my life and in the lives of those close to me should be of little concern to a reader of a novel; and two, my silence served to prolong the discussion, thus keeping the book on certain lists for longer than expected. But few people anymore care about the blue exploits of this old dallier, so I'll say this: it is a work of fiction. If the events of *The Imagists* had occurred I would have written them as nonfiction. I have written one memoir (focused, I see now, on the writing life—what a hypocrite I am) and essays on literature and art and beauty, as well as one on minimalism, that couch-cushion fart of a movement. I've written articles on Oldenburg and Rauschenberg and Jasper Johns for *Artforum* and *ARTnews*. This is all to say that I do not have a problem with writing the real. I will leave it to biographers—should any interest remain—to produce a detailed catalogue of my post-adolescence, but for now suffice it to say that the events of the book did not happen, not exactly.

While I did, like Hal, move to Chicago from Ohio in the waning days of the 1960s, I was not, as Hal is for the first two months of the book's chronology, homeless (well, not for more than a night or two at a stretch). When I arrived at the gloomy majesty of Union Station I was greeted by a cousin of mine who didn't quite know what she'd let into her life. I overstayed my welcome in her Hyde Park apartment by a good four months. I ate her food while she attended classes at the U of C. I tried to sleep with her friends (and, I admit, one drunk night, *her*). She tolerated me with what I see now was near superhuman patience. Eventually I lied my way into a job as a line cook at a greasy spoon and then as a handyman at a gallery where I learned to light the shows of too many painters I felt were below me (I was nearly uniformly wrong about that), and a few who I admired greatly. I moved into a one-room flat in the Ukrainian Village neighborhood, an apartment I'd stay in for the next three years.

In the book, Hal has had no training. He works with an innate knowledge in his hands and eyes. I myself had gotten good, though not great, marks as a student at the School of the Art Institute, where I enrolled my second year in the city. In critiques my teachers spoke of potential, though none were all that impressed with my compositions, which were by and large bad abstracts. My fellow sub-pars and I were defined in two groups: the meek who wanted to make what they thought was "proper" art (which almost invariably meant some spin on Impressionism), and those (including myself) who wanted to eschew all rules and create something terribly new, which really just meant that we were too lazy to spend the hours at figure drawing or even color theory. The result for the first group was work that, while perhaps proficient on a craft level, lacked any imagination. We mavericks on the other hand, churned out canvas after canvas of muddied and formless dreck. While my occasional piece might have offered a spark of inspiration, that was overshadowed by my fundamental misunderstanding of the nature of visual communication.

Of course, I didn't know any of this at the time. I rolled my eyes at my classmates' fumbling attempts to extract meaning from my work. I spent my nights in dive bars with other artists, all of us as proud of the array of hues crusted in our cuticles as we would have been the scars of some noble war. We were a tribe, we young turks of the scene, all ready to set the art world ablaze. And a couple would, in their own small ways. Most of us, though, would either continue to create in obscurity, or give up and try our hands at something different. So it was, is, and ever shall be.

During my third year of school, my brother Lucas joined me in Chicago. I should say straight away that Lucas is the aforementioned absence from my oeuvre. If you look back on my books, there is nary a brother to be found. There have been drafts where he makes an appearance in one form or another, but no finished product features his likeness. (And for you archivists waiting for me to shuffle off, I have never been in the habit of keeping these early drafts.) This, I suppose, is his long overdue debut, and though I have no hope of doing him justice, he is, I realize now, the reason for this rambling and otherwise unnecessary prologue.

We grew up on a small dairy farm outside of Dayton, an operation barely kept afloat over the years by government subsidies and frugal living. Our father and his antiquated ways could not keep up with the rising trend of factory farming. Father's outfit was organic before organic was a term, a farming practice born out of nothing more than an utter lack of business sense. Lucas was younger than I by four years. Through our respective teenage years we tended to the girls, as Father referred to the three dozen cows we held, feeding twice a day, slogging through mud and manure, the stench of the animals and their waste weaving its way into our clothes and branding itself onto our skin. No matter; most other boys at our school carried with them the same olfactory residue (or worse—those poor pig farmers' sons). This might seem a pastoral existence looking back from the brave new nightmare of GMOs and cage-farming we live in now, but at the time

I had little conception of any of that. All I knew was that I hated it. I hated the land and the slow, stupid cows, and I hated Father and every other man of the town for what I saw as the smallness of their thoughts. I saw them shuffling from the feed store to the tractor supply to the café, slump-shouldered and monosyllabic. I saw them all—Father included— look at me sideways whenever I accidentally verbalized my artistic ambitions or was caught admiring too long the sunset over the fields.

Who rejected whom first would never be answered. Facts of the past slip away into constellations, forever subject to interpretation. But words? Ah, words will dig their serif'd fingers into gray matter and take hold. One night we sat in our living room, the radio playing quietly in the corner. I was fifteen. Father looked up from his Sears farming catalogue and said to me, "You get yourself a girl. Ask one of them little things from school to go out to the pictures. And you make sure some folks see you." The implication was clear enough. I can see now that he said this for my own sake as well as his own, that he saw this as a part of his job as a father, to teach me the ways of being a man in the world. But it only served to reify my discontent. From the time I was able to imagine a place outside of our farm and Dayton, I dreamed of getting out.

Lucas came to Chicago with little save for his usual generous spirit and an old Nikon box camera. I hadn't seen him in three years. Upon his disembarking the train we embraced as we never had before. He was taller than he'd been when I last saw him, and broader. His hair shagged over his ears. Out on the street I flipped the collar of my Navy coat up against the wind and Lucas did the same with his beat-up old brown barn parka. I was overcome with relief that he had left behind the life of the plodding farmhand, and that we could now, together, begin our lives.

And of course I was delighted that he'd taken on a hobby such as photography, so with materials pilfered from various departments around the school, we built a darkroom in a corner of our apartment (an addition my landlord surely would have objected to, had I ever actually met the man), a space with what I know now must have had dangerously insufficient ventilation. But despite the shoddy equipment, Lucas's aptitude with the camera was clear from the first prints. He took a job at a developer and spent his off time riding the El end to end, disembarking wherever the tableau caught his eye, and snapping stills.

This is not to paint the kid as an innocent. We were brothers after all. The predilections of one become the habits of the other, or some such equation.

Now Tasha I'll get to in a moment. But first, let's talk about the other women. Hal, you'll find out soon enough, has experiences with a rather long string of women throughout the greater Chicago area, as well as one or two in Wisconsin. These scenes are all, to one degree or another, if not autobiographical in the strictest sense of the word, then certainly created with a notable level of education behind them. Through my twenties I was profoundly and inexplicably successful with women. I can say this with little fear of being seen as a braggart now that that success is a mere speck in my past, ever nearing the vanishing point. I craved women constantly. Their skin, their voices, their gaits, their briefest of underthings. I wanted to devour them. I was so preoccupied with them that now, looking back, it is a wonder that I was able to finish any paintings, even ones as slapdash as mine.

Luckily for me, my brother turned out to be as adept as myself when last call came around. Plus, he had a youthful wholesomeness about him to which women responded. I and most other men I knew had developed a film over us, an emulsion of paint thinner, sweat, and secreted whiskey that formed a sort of paste which was, if not actually visible, then certainly odorous and ever-present. Lucas, though, despite his hours in the darkroom, and the fact that neither of us spent too much time in the shower at the end of the hall, always appeared unsullied.

For a week during my final year at the Art Institute, the department brought in Henry Worthe, who we all admired either for his work in the realm of abstract expressionism or the money he made off that work, or both. We showed him a series of three paintings each, along with a written artist's statement. He critiqued my work, using words like "primitive" and "reductive," words that I somehow in my arrogance and idiocy took as compliments. Later at a bar, as we hopelessly poor students bought round after round of drinks for the man, he put a small, dry hand on my shoulder and said to me, "I liked your statement. You've got a way with words. Your paintings are shit, but you're a good writer." I didn't know which implication I hated more: that I had no knack for the canvas, or that my real talent might lie in something so pedestrian as the written word.

The first piece of writing I had published was a letter to the editor in *ARTnews*. Those of us who stuck around the city after school had started exploring new styles and subject matter. Our works began taking on more figures, as well as more of what we saw as social import. In part this was a reaction to the political climate—Vietnam was still happening and Watergate was in full swing—but also to what we decided was a sort of stagnancy and hollowness in the more established corners of the art world. We'd grown tired of trying to be New York. We began to embrace our Chicago-ness. We were the stockyards. We were the elder Daley and the '68 convention (though none of us had actually been there). We were so many sweaty summers on the lakefront. Our work became surreal and grotesque, often cartoonish. Meat became a recurrent motif, as well as severed limbs and outsized genitalia. It meant to disturb, to challenge the integrity of our viewers' stomachs. It was not pleasant to look at. In my letter to *ARTnews*, I spoke of the emptiness of what was still being hailed as new. I spoke of what art could be, a visual microphone for the injustices and systemic inequalities of the world. I alluded to the artists around the world that were using their work as a soapbox (implicitly including myself and my cohorts in the group), while they at the magazine still thought we should be wowed by Warhol's Brillos. I fully expected to have my missive ignored, but not only was it printed, but they contacted me about writing a short piece on the Chicago scene. Thusly, my writing career began, though I hardly knew it then.

Lucas shot the paintings (which did not include my own) featured in that story, and in the process got a sidebar of his city work in those pages. What he captured in those photographs was a city I had never seen before. Yes, he got the grit that we'd all latched onto in our own work—the Southside poverty, the factory smog, the desperate river fishermen— but he captured it all with the admiration of an outsider, of a young man who found grace in just about everything he saw. It was remarkable, a lens into humanity itself. Some of my cohorts would refer to Lucas as my "project," as if I had been guiding him into the world, advising him, teaching him the tenuous rules of composition. But, no. His was the untrained genius, the innate sense of space and form, with which I imbued the character of Hal. It was, as they say, a God-given talent. I knew even then that I had nothing to do with it.

Soon he was being contacted by galleries through the city. He was put in group shows, his work blown up and mounted, often on the coveted back wall, the centerpiece of the evening. Within a year of his humble arrival from little old Dayton, he was the first among us to get a solo show. He and I arrived at the Meyer Gallery on Diversey, and surveyed the room: his work pinned to the walls, the simplicity of the mounting a perfect complement to the easy brilliance of the photos. The turn-out was larger than either of us had expected. I watched as the owner hurriedly slapped a wad of cash into her assistant's hand and sent him out for more wine. That kid, I thought: not too different from myself. And then there was my little brother. A sold-out show.

The gallery owner, a rail-thin brunette half looped on white wine and unforeseen profit, came up to Lucas, put both hands on either side of his face and said, "They love you. You can have everything." This might have been a case of well intentioned hyperbole, but compared to the rest of us, myself and my friends, many of whom began to ache with envy and mask that feeling with increasingly self-righteous contempt for the fickle bourgeois art establishment, Lucas did seem to be boarding a great and mysterious cruise liner while we were anchored to a pier of obscurity.

—

Now, finally: Tasha. She was Lucas's girl. Or rather, she is based loosely on Lucas's girl, who prefers not to be named in these pages, and so whom I will refer to as S.

Lucas met S at the Berghoff, where she was working as a hostess. She was a lovely girl—intelligent, happy, unassumingly beautiful—and she came into our lives like a cleansing rain. I say "our lives" because though she and Lucas were the official item, we were a trio to the point that others took to calling Lucas and me *Jules et Jim*. Unlike us, though, S was Chicago through and through. Grew up in Pilsen. Daughter of an honest-to-God meatpacker. Did two years at DePaul studying accounting before dropping out due to what she referred to as her "Kafka-esque ennui." Her mere presence tore holes in the identities that I, and to a lesser extent Lucas, had spent years developing. And we loved her for it. Each time she exposed some small ignorance of the city, we took it as a challenge to live more honestly, to be ourselves and to know the place more deeply. It was just the opposite of what should have happened. Had anyone else done this, pointed out where we'd taken shortcuts in our quest to be to artistic spokespeople for the place, we probably would have excommunicated them from the group. We certainly wouldn't have gone out of our way to envelop them into our lives, as we did with S. But her honesty won us over. Not just honesty with others—in which case she might have just been another insufferable critic, and Lord knows we had enough of those—but honesty with herself. She was a constant introspector. She would happily announce over our meager breakfasts that she'd suddenly realized she'd been an inadequate older sister, or that she would never be able to truly appreciate opera, or that so-and-so was far more in tune with the spiritual world than she. Lucas and I began joining her in these revelation-confessions. In our dark apartment I'd say, "I've never read one word of the Bible."

Lucas would counter with, "I'm constantly afraid of dying."

S would say, "If I could have only one taste for the rest of my life, it would be deviled egg."

Before you ask: no, I did not sleep with her. Rather, before you reach a certain part in the novel (which will begin as soon as this introduction concludes (should it ever—the prospect is feeling increasingly in doubt)) and begin to foment your own connections between what I am telling here and what transpires between the characters, I ask that you trust me this once: even I who once tried to make it with my cousin had some standards, plastic and ill-defined as they were.

We were happy around S. We were quite happy in general. Lucas continued to hone his craft. He invested in a Leica, and we found an enormous, run-down hovel in Humboldt Park. S all but moved in with us, only occasionally venturing back to her studio in Edgewater for fresh clothes or to pick up her bills. The new place had two bathrooms, one of which we made into a slightly more proper space for Lucas to develop his pictures. Each time I went in there I was astonished at the images he captured. It is useless to try to describe the way they made my heart lurch. His was a rare combination of talent and compassion. His one monograph, published by a local art press and entitled *Shared Chicago*, still pops up in used book stores every once in a while. It is an item worth hunting for.

I wrote more articles for small art magazines, reluctantly accepting my knack for sentences and slowly reducing the time and energy I put into painting. I also started playing around with stories. I suppose it was during this time that I first had the idea for *The Imagists*, though I wouldn't actually begin writing it for some months and whatever nascent notions had been in my head then bore little resemblance to what would be the finished book five years on. I was, though, starting to be able to imagine myself as something other than a painter. I wish I could look back on the embryonic days of this career and recall excitement and passion, but what I felt most was resignation. The last painting I would complete was of the living room of that place in Humboldt.

At our urging, S took a position answering phones at the Meyer Gallery, where Lucas held his first solo, and was quickly promoted to assistant to the director and became known through the community as a person who could *get things done*. Everyone we knew saw what was happening. With the connections S made at the gallery and Lucas' growing reputation, the two of them were quickly moving beyond our scrappy beginnings. They were getting personal invitations to the city's biggest openings. They began slipping off to dinners and would, only after being pressed upon returning home, admit that they'd been with such-and-such painter or sculptor or gallery owner.

In September 1976, we got a call from our father, asking that we come home for our mother's birthday. By that time I had realized that I did not in fact hate the place, only pitied the people who lived there—which might be worse. I attempted to beg off, but Lucas insisted that we all go. For some reason I could not fathom, he wanted to show S the farm. The three of us drove to Ohio the next day. We picked up that cousin of ours, the one with whom I stayed upon my arrival in the city and who had seldom spoken to me since. She'd become a lawyer, news we'd heard by way of letters from our mother. She tucked herself against the passenger door while I drove and Lucas and S leaned into each other in the backseat. We smoked cigarettes and ate oranges that the cousin brought while Lucas spoke excitedly about home.

"When it rains," he said, "you can smell all of the colors of the place. The green of the grass. The brown of the mud. Even the white paint on the porch."

It occurred to me that my brother and I might have had very different lives back in Ohio. He always blended in with the town's men better than I did, and was in turn more accepted. But, of course, it might have been that he did not, as I did, look down upon them and Father for their middle-American ways. He seemed to genuinely enjoy the bland food and wordless conversations. The silence between Father and me was less carefree. As the years went on, as my adolescence developed, the silences between us lengthened and deepened. He didn't understand my ambitions, and I showed no respect for the life he'd chosen to live.

This was the first time I'd been back since leaving. The place was largely the same, though the paint appeared a little more chipped, perhaps, and the gravel drive was empty of bikes and balls, those trappings of boyhood. Our mother came out to meet us, descended the porch steps with her arms out and her face smiling and wet with tears. She went to Lucas first, then me, then S, whom she'd never met before, kissing us all. That was Mother. For further insight into the woman, see *every mother character I've ever written*. But in the meantime I'll say this: she had a heart that pumped love like an open hydrant. She'd nearly made growing up there bearable for me. She brought us into the house, where we encountered our myriad uncles and aunts and cousins, all of whom embraced us and led us further into the house to where they'd laid out a spread of food that could have fed all of our compatriots back in Chicago for a week. And the party wasn't until the next day.

For Mother's sake, Lucas gave S his old room and slept on the couch. I spent the next few nights in my room amidst the smell of the cows and the ghosts of my past.

The party was an assembly of generations of farm people. They settled themselves into the folding chairs, wiping hay fever from their noses and eyes with handkerchiefs. The young ones ran in and out of the old house, toddlers laughing at their own movements through space. Nearly the entire town was at the house. More food: ham, casseroles, Jell-o, baskets of rolls. From the living room I looked out the window at Lucas and S as they strolled the pastures arm-in-arm. My aunts brought out a sheet cake and Mother insisted that the little children help her blow out the candles.

That evening, after everyone had left, Lucas asked me to join him in the barn. The cows were resting, breathing shallow bursts of air from their wet snouts. Lucas said to me, "We're going to stay. We talked about it and we're going to stay here and help run the farm."

I didn't understand. "For how long?"

"Forever," he said. "Or until we do something else. But for a good long while anyway."

I smiled. "You're feeling sentimental. That's all. Jesus, as soon as we get back to the city, you're not going to want to leave."

"We're not coming back," he said. "Not at all. I have money saved up for the next couple months' rent, enough time for you to find a roommate or a new place. I know I won't want to leave. That's not the life we want, neither of us."

"I forbid it," I said, trying lamely to wrest control of the situation.

Lucas smiled. "I knew you wouldn't be happy about it." He looked down at the ground, said, "We're going to have a kid. Found out a couple weeks ago. We're getting married."

I suddenly saw him devolving into one of those marble-mouthed simpletons I'd known all my life, one of the morons in John Deere caps that had inhabited our parents' house all afternoon. And what of S? Given over to baking and cleaning and child-rearing. And worst of all, the child: how lucky I'd been to escape the morass of boorish traditions and philistine customs that permeated the world of my youth. Would the child have such luck to desire something more? Surely the chances would be better with Lucas and S at the helm of his upbringing, but there were too many variables, too much risk. Was I a snob? Yes. Unquestionably, yes. But that snobbishness was born out of a genuine suffocation, a personal history where I saw individuality and expression—those things that I valued above all else—squashed. I could not imagine how my brother could be satisfied with the life of a dairy farmer, for himself or a family.

"What are you going to do," I said, "take pictures of the fucking cows?"

"Maybe," he said. "I don't know if I'll take pictures anymore."

And then I hit him. With as much force as I could muster—which in all likelihood was not that much, as I was a relatively weak young man—I struck him in the face with my right fist closed. He fell back to the dirt and held his jaw and looked as if his eyes were swimming. A few of the nearby cows looked at us. I leaned over and said, "I will never speak to you again." I repeated myself and expanded. "I will never speak to you again if you stay here as a fucking dairy farmer. If you stop taking pictures, and milk cows for the rest of your life, you will no longer have a brother."

What audacity to present such an ultimatum. What heartlessness. And yet I did not back down. I went to my childhood room and sat sleeplessly on the bed, alternately enraged and overcome with a feeling of desolation. The next morning I waited by the car. "What's going on?" my cousin said. I ignored her. When my watch hit nine o'clock, the time we'd all appointed for departure, I opened the car door. At one minute past, I got in, said, "Let's go," to the cousin. She settled into her seat apprehensively and we drove the width of Indiana in silence.

—

I sold the prints that Lucas had left hanging in the bathroom. Brought them to the Meyer Gallery and told the tiny brunette that Lucas was back home tending to family business and that he wanted me to act as his emissary in the meantime. She said she'd gotten a letter from S saying that she wouldn't be returning. She put those prints up and they sold and I paid the next three months' rent and bought myself a heavy wool overcoat for the upcoming winter. Then I went into Lucas' darkroom and developed a roll of film that he had not gotten around to before—as I saw it—abandoning me. I'd spent enough time in there with him that I'd learned the basic techniques. Even in the dark I could tell they were exquisite. In the light, after they'd set, I saw clearly the faces of children, one after another: laughing and crying, dirty and fresh, beatific and doleful. I'd never known Lucas to focus his work this way, to train his lens on one subject. I found another roll and developed those and discovered another sequence of small faces, this one perhaps even more heartrending than the last. I tacked a length of twine across the living room, hung each print, and walked back and forth in front of them like an animal in a zoo, my anger growing with each pass. How could he give this up? How could he turn his back on his own talent like it was a mere hobby? Of course I know better now what I was feeling. It was not only envy of his great abilities or even righteous indignation over his denying the world access to the product of his eye. It was jealousy born out of the knowledge that he chose the farm over me. He chose the life that that our father offered over the one I gave to him. He chose, ultimately, the world that never accepted me. Sure, yes, I was the one to leave Ohio, but Ohio had made it all too easy.

By that point the rumors were flying. Lucas was dead. Lucas and S were in Europe. Lucas was going to debut something any day now, something extraordinary. I refused to answer gossip, but I knew that Lucas' work was too recognizable in Chicago. The new series would raise more questions, ones I wouldn't be able to smirk and shrug off. I packed some clothes and Lucas' prints and negatives, tried to collect on a few debts from friends, and scanned the Greyhound schedule, found a place about as far from Ohio as could be.

Should I tell you how that Midwestern boy felt upon first seeing San Francisco? The Pacific Ocean? Shall I attempt to articulate the sense of precarious freedom that the edge of the world provided him? How he wept at the sight of that great bridge, how he climbed the Headlands on the far side and scanned the water and the city with its banks of fog, that place for which it seems the word *vista* might have been first enunciated? Shall I describe to you the scent of eucalyptus and how that boy felt the molecules bloat his lungs and take root within him?

No. Those are the happy details of an altogether different mythology. The beauty of the Bay has been extolled enough, and anyway there are crimes to be confessed. Let's instead discuss how that boy entered the first gallery he found and introduced himself with his brother's name, how he laid his brother's prints on a desk and claimed them as his own. Let's focus on how that gallery owner jumped at the sight of them. "Amazing," he said. He used other words. *Divine. Magnificent.* "Where did you come from?" he asked, in awe of the faces looking up at him.

So I got my first solo show. I'd only given the owner one set of prints and so when he asked for more, I said, "Give me a month," and holed up in a rundown motel, the other set waiting patiently beneath the mattress on which I slept and ate and drank and communed with a number of young San Franciscans. The city knew me as Lucas and I answered without hesitation at the mention of his name. I spent Thanksgiving in a bar and brought a sad girl with a heroin habit back to my room. I showed her Lucas' work while she shot up, spread it out across the floor. She said she'd never seen anything so beautiful, and I knew that it wasn't the dope talking.

By the night of the show I'd almost convinced myself that the work was mine, that I'd somehow earned the accolades I was surely about to receive. I walked thirteen blocks to the gallery, stopping at the top of each hill to catch my breath. The sky was clear and the ocean wafted over me on the wind. I spent this time as I had every waking minute since I left Chicago: making sense of what I was doing. I told myself that if the son of a bitch wouldn't take it himself, I'd have it, all of it: the attention, the money, the validation. At the gallery, before going in, I watched through the window as people were already huddled in front of the mounted photographs, whispering to one another, smiling, slowly bringing hands to faces in near disbelief at the beauty captured before them. Where would their love go if I were not to take it? I'd let their praise soak into me like watercolor into paper.

Inside the gallery the evening passed like a dream. As might occur in a dream, the Midwestern boy was two people at once. He was artist and criminal. He was guest of honor and trespasser. And what does the boy do when pride and guilt collide? He shakes hands. He smiles and laughs and sips wine and never lets on that he is not who he claims to be, that he has never created anything of worth in his life. Mere days later he collects his money, twelve thousand, and smells someone else's sweat and genius on those bills. He breaks down, spends the next two weeks alone in his room, denying himself both the distracting pleasures of company and the numbing anesthesia of drugs and booze. He begins to write. He composes the first line of what will be his novel: "Hal wanted to be celebrated."

—

The Imagists went on to win a number of prizes and was alternately lauded and reviled for its "frank treatment of sexuality"—a treatment that no doubt seems downright abstemious by today's standards. The book has remained in print all this time and has been translated into more languages than I can remember. In the past quarter-century, Hal's hubris-fueled fall from the heights of fame and adoration has sparked enough Icarus and Faustus references to drive prep school literature professors to consider the lucrative field of data entry. And Tasha's unwavering commitment to her man despite his many infidelities has provided women's studies departments with further evidence of the "masturbatory fantasies of late-20th century American male novelists" (yes, words stick in such a mind as mine). To many readers the mention of these characters has come to reference artistic devotion, the dangers of success, and (not to let on too much for those of you who have yet to thumb through the final movements of the story itself) the resilience of the human heart. Yet when I have had occasion to look at it over the past two-and-a-half decades, it calls to mind none of these things. Nor am I reminded of moments of critical and commercial triumph or even the sensation of satisfaction I'm sure I must have felt at times during the writing process. Instead, the book has always seemed more like the work of some twisted poet, an erasure project in which all references to love and fraternity have been wiped away.

Six months after returning to Chicago from California, I ran into a friend who'd been holding a letter for me. It was from S and said that my father had died not long after my mother's birthday. He went as I imagine he'd have preferred: out in the barn, tending to the girls. It also said that they'd heard about the sale of Lucas' work at the Meyer Gallery and the show in California. He wanted me to keep the proceeds in gratitude for all I'd done for him. I did not respond. Forgiveness can be the cruelest punishment. Decades elapsed and eventually there were days when I did not think about Lucas or S, but they have been rare.

Then, earlier this year, I was contacted by my cousin, the lawyer, who is now partnered in a small practice in the west suburbs and whom I run into from time to time. She directed me to an article in *ARTnews* alerting its readers to an upcoming show at Chicago's Museum of Contemporary Photography, an exhibit that would showcase a certain photographer whose work has not been displayed since the mid-1970s. The show, entitled *Touch*, would examine the connections between humans and animals, as well as birth and death, and focused most closely on life on a small Ohio dairy farm. The article included one photograph, a close-up of a cow, her mouth open in mid-low. So, he did it. I would have recognized his work anywhere. Time is not the villain folks like to make it out to be. Rather, it is the most effective of mentors. I am a fifty-six-year-old man, married with two children, a list of books to my name, and little connection to my beginnings. So I went to the show.

Each photograph was framed in simple black. The cow I'd seen in the article took up the far wall, the centerpiece, her big black cow eyes cast in my direction as I entered. If anything, Lucas' talent has advanced, his relationship with the subject both deeper and more purely articulated. There were animals feeding, playing, sleeping. They were giving birth and being slaughtered. The camera's eye was not a foreigner in the landscape. Rather, its presence felt as vital as the very moments of life being recorded.

I saw him almost immediately, standing towards a corner with S. He looked older, but lean and robust. He wore what looked to be a new suit. His hair was thinning. S was beautiful as ever, breathtakingly so. They stood, each with an arm around the other's waist, speaking with another woman, an old Chicago socialite type sipping champagne. S and the woman broke off from Lucas, and his eyes found me. I approached and we said hello. "You look good," I said.

"I'm bald," he said, running a hand over his sparsely occupied pate.

I set a hand on my stomach. "I'm fat."

And so our reunion began not with words of apology or mentions of the past, but with brief admissions of our middle-age vanities and insecurities.

Since then I've met Lucas' children and he mine. He and S invited my family and me to the farm, where we spent a long weekend, my girls—seventeen and fourteen—engrossed in the muddy mess of it all, neither of them able to imagine that their old man had grown up in such a world. Lucas' son helps run the place. A tall, muscular, good-looking young man, he sent my daughters into states of coy muteness. Intelligent, too, that one. And S, she seems to have taken to farm life like I never could have imagined. She seems utterly at home, content. Late one night I tried to offer her and Lucas the money I stole from them through his work, but of course they refused. I am still trying to find a way to make amends.

Upon returning from Ohio to our home in Winnetka, I started a new novel, my ninth (though that hardly seems possible). This one is loosely based on the story of Castor and Pollux, sons of Leda. In the version of the myth I prefer, the former is fathered by a mortal and the latter by Zeus, king of the gods. The brothers are inseparable until one, Castor, is fatally wounded in battle. Pollux, the divine brother, unable to live without Castor, strikes a deal with the gods to allow them both to live on as the constellation Gemini, the twins. A fable of sorts, I do not predict this book will sell well. Yet I write it anyway.

I've also begun painting again. My hands show the first signs of arthritis as I stretch the canvases, but the discomfort dissipates as I set my brush to the empty plane and happily lose myself in the creation of truly terrible art.

A Dry Season

My father was a farmer, waking before light and spending his days trying to guide and control the life that came out of the earth. The farm belonged to his family gone back three generations, corn from the get-go. My mother stayed at home and had us children because we lived in the world and that was the way of it. In my very early years my mother was a lively woman. She took us out in the old Ford truck, pushing and pulling the shifter with such vigor I was in awe of the machine, that it did not fall apart under her power. But then, in my ninth year of life, she stopped taking us into town, leaving the job to my father or Robert, our farmhand, or even from time to time Robert's wife, Estelle. Soon, my mother stopped leaving the property and then one day she stopped leaving the house altogether.

We lived just outside of a town called Sycamore. Seventy miles from Chicago, due west. I was the second and last child for my parents. My sister was Harriet. I was the one, though, that our parents had been waiting for—a boy—and it showed in the way they treated me, taking my side in fights between Harriet and me, giving me a stern talking-to for something that would have surely gotten Harriet a spanking or worse.

From an early age I understood myself to be different from my sister.

One summer day, Harriet and I found ourselves, as we often did on summer days, bored enough to act like friends. We scratched hopscotch into the ground by the barn, but quickly tired of it. We tried to get our dog, a black Labrador named Petal, to chase a stick, but she wasn't budging from the shade of the house. It was too hot and she was too old. We sat down next to her just as our father came out of the barn leading Grace, his best mare. She had a hitch in one of her back legs. "Goddamn it," our father said. "What the shit." Then he called out loudly for Robert. "Go on and play somewhere else," he said to us, waving his hand in no particular direction. "Robert!" he called again.

Harriet and I went behind the barn and peered around the corner. Robert came out of the house, where he'd been having his lunch. His wife was there that day. Estelle often visited with my mother, sometimes bringing vegetables or flowers from her garden. It was easy to forget that Robert worked for our father; most of the time they seemed like partners or even brothers—Father being the elder, of course. Estelle followed Robert out of the house, but stayed on the porch, leaning against the whitewashed post, watching her husband and our father. Robert shuffled over to where our father had Grace's leg up, examining her hoof.

"What the hell did you do to this shoeing?" our father said.

"I had a little trouble with that one," Robert said, matter-of-fact. He stuck his hands on his back pockets.

"I can see that. What I can't see is how you were gonna reimburse me the price of a healthy mare after she goes lame 'cause of your half-assed work."

It wasn't like our father to talk to him that way. Robert's body slumped a little, but then he stood up straighter than normal. "I don't think it's quite that bad, Karl, come on. She'll be back to normal in a couple days."

Our father looked at him. "Well, then we can laugh about it in a couple days, but for now all I got is a lame horse." He turned his eyes back to Grace's hoof. "Christ," he said. "How short d'you cut this?"

Harriet and I headed out across the field, moving carefully through the rows of tender cornstalks that we could have trampled with one misstep. The stalks should have been higher by that point in July, but we'd been suffering a hot and dry spell that was dwarfing everything. The sun was high and I had to squint to get any detail from the wash of green and brown and white in front of me. "Shoo-wee," Harriet said, referring to either the heat or the interaction between our father and Robert.

"No kidding," I said. Either way.

Harriet was twelve. I would be ten in the fall. She was already showing signs of having our mother's tall and lean physique. She towered over my short, chubby self. Every once in a while I would have to double-time a few steps to catch up to her.

"What do you think Dad's got a bug about?" I asked.

"Well, it isn't just Gracie," Harriet said. "Even I know that hoof'll grow out in a few days."

"You think he just woke up on the wrong side of the bed?"

"I'll let you know as soon as I figure out how to read minds," she said.

"Come on."

Harriet breathed loudly.

The field sloped ever so slightly downward to a line of anemic sycamores. For the longest time I thought the town had been named after this meager grouping, not knowing they dotted the whole region. Past the trees the ground fell away and we slid and hopped down to the creek bed that edged the south border of our land. The east and west sides ran into the McClendon and Wilson farms, and to the north was the gravel county road that took us into town.

The creek bed was made of smooth, rounded stones, settled enough that they held in place as we stepped. There should have been water, at least a little, for another three weeks. A few days before, I had been walking the field and I found my father standing at the creek's edge. He looked down at it and then up at the cloudless sky. He took his brown cap off his head and used it to shield his eyes from the sun. I approached and asked him what he was doing and he looked back down at the creek and said, "Minding the store."

"You think Mom's ever gonna come out?" I asked Harriet. Our mother hadn't been past the front threshold in seven months at that point.

"Like I said, if get to read minds, I'll let you know."

"If I was Dad I'd make her go out. She's his wife. She has to listen to him."

"I'm going back," she said abruptly, and made for the bank of the creek.

"Don't," I said.

She stopped. "Don't what?"

"Don't go yet."

"Don't go yet, what?"

I got it and rolled my eyes. "Don't go yet *please*."

She came back and we resumed our progress along the edge of our property.

"You can't make a person do anything," Harriet said.

"Kevin McClendon made Shane Wilson eat a worm," I said. This incident had happened, to the other boys' disgust and delight, just before school let out for the summer.

"That's not the same thing," she said. "Anyway, he didn't have to do it."

"Kevin was going to beat him up if he didn't."

"Yeah," she said, "so he could have taken the beating."

"I bet I could make you do something," I said.

"This is not a game I want to play." She was making a serious effort to sound like an adult in those days. "Just stop," she said, "or I'm heading back to the house."

"I bet—"

"Stop!" she almost screamed.

I slowed and let Harriet take the lead and then bent down and picked up a small stone. I tossed it, not hard, and it tapped her on the head, right on the part in her hair, where it split into pigtails.

"Ow!" she said, reaching back to rub the spot. "God, what was that for?"

She waited for an answer, but I said nothing. Then Harriet puffed out a breath and clambered up the embankment. She strode quickly back toward the house, but I didn't try to catch up. I often wonder what would have happened if I'd called her name one more time, if I said it with the right tone to communicate what I was feeling down beneath my too-many layers of childish solipsism. Would she have turned around if she'd known—if I'd known—how scared I was, how sad, how angry with our mother and father I had grown to be, how utterly confused I was by the world around us? Would she have come back to me? Perhaps. But I said nothing. Only watched as she got smaller and smaller in the distance.

—

When I got back to the house the radio in the living room was on. Tchaikovsky. The only station in our area played Tchaikovsky every afternoon at one o'clock. And every day my mother would turn it on and raise the volume until the speaker buzzed and then go upstairs into her room. We got to know the composer's work well. Even from outside we'd hear it. When the piece was over, she'd come back down looking puffy in the face. None of us would say what we knew: that for some reason our mother went upstairs each afternoon and cried to Tchaikovsky. Years later I would read a biography of the composer and learn that he suffered from serious depression through his life, as did his own mother. Rumors have floated ever since his death that he actually took his own life, that the story that he'd been overcome by cholera was a cover up to preserve his reputation. Unsubstantiated, but not out of the realm of possibility. He was troubled, after all.

I once asked my father why he'd married my mother and he shrugged and said, "It was time." Nothing about her—only the moment when he thought it would be right to take a wife. And so there we all were. If my family had lived in a later time and different place, we might have had words to correspond with what ailed my mother, terms that are so easily accessible in our current cultural lexicon: depression, agoraphobia, panic disorder. We would have had her treated by a doctor who would suggest more than "a few good nights of rest" and "plenty of water," as the doc from town had. She could have been given a series of serotonin inhibitors and been enrolled in talk therapy. But back then and back there we were at a loss, perhaps most of all myself, who only knew that there was something wrong with her.

That day on the farm, my father came into the house just after me. Normally he would have just gone to do the work that took him farthest from the house, not returning until the music softened. But this day he walked straight to the radio and turned the dial until it clicked. Barely a beat passed before my mother issued a piercing scream from upstairs. Even after traveling through the bedroom door, down the stairs, and across the room, it was still enough to jerk my hands up to my ears. Our dad took the stairs two at a time while I tried to block that voice from my head. It was almost unbearable for the second that the bedroom door was open. But it didn't end. She stopped to reload her lungs and then once again bombarded the house. Every few seconds she would silence herself and our dad would plead angrily, and then the noise would resume. Finally he came slowly down the stairs, looking hollowed out. He went to the radio and turned it up even louder than before.

"Dad?" I said, over the crescendo of strings. I wasn't sure what I wanted to say, to ask. Something about my mother, about adults.

"Is it important?" he said. I said nothing. "Later, then." He went through the screen door and then stopped. "Robert's in town tending to some business," he said. "Make sure the horses got water in their buckets."

He drove the truck to the far side of the field. There he got out and looked west to the Wilson farm. Two white arcs hung low over their fields. In recent years, many farmers had installed irrigation sprinklers. The Wilsons had done this the year before and recorded a banner harvest. This season, with the non-irrigated farms like ours suffering from the drought, they were practically set to do us in.

I dragged the hose through the barn to fill up the horses' water buckets. My father or Robert would have taken the buckets out to where the spigot was, but I knew that if I was able to lift the bucket, it wasn't enough to get the horses through the afternoon. I reached the hose through the gate of Grace's stall and watched the bucket fill. Then I pulled the hose back, placed a thumb over the stream, and shot a quick burst at Grace's rump. Her head shot up and a shake passed down her neck and withers. She looked at me, the whites of her eyes showing. I gave her another shot and she whinnied. When I was done I found Harriet and Estelle back behind the house. My sister was perched on a sawhorse, her ankles wrapped around the legs to balance. The music was still wailing through the open windows.

Estelle turned to me and said, "Well, there you are." I read her lips as much as I heard her. "How are you doing, sweetie?" Harriet looked at me with some kind of sad contempt. "Come on over here," Estelle said. I went to her and she put her hand on my shoulder. "You know your mama's just having a hard time, right? She's gonna pop right out of this just as soon as she can." It was clear that Estelle wanted it to be true, that she liked Harriet and me and our mother a great deal, and that she did want good things for our family. She was a decent sort of woman and I knew I should have felt comforted, but having this smiling face tell me that my mother was going to be okay only made it seem more uncertain. I looked up at her and waited for something further, but all she did was purse her lips into a tighter smile and tilt her head slightly to the side.

"If you ever need anything," she said, "if you ever need *anything*, you tell Estelle and I will just come running." She looked at my sister. "That goes for both of you. You say the word and I will be here." She pushed a lock of hair away from Harriet's face and behind her ear. "In fact," she said, "maybe we can go get some ice cream later."

Harriet smiled and just then the music went mute. Our mother appeared in the living room window, her face slightly grayed behind the screen. "Staying for dinner, Estelle?" she said. Her eyes moved to Harriet and then to me before landing on Estelle.

"Oh, I don't know. I'm not sure how long Robert's gonna be. Anyway, I don't want to put you out."

"I'll make enough just in case—chicken tonight," our mother said, and looked at me, as this was my favorite. Then she disappeared back into the house.

Estelle raised her eyebrows and said to us, "Doesn't that sound good."

—

Harriet went inside to help our mother with dinner, and with Robert gone and my father off in the fields, I was again on my own. I thought about heading over to see what Shane Wilson was up to, maybe cooling off under his dad's field sprinklers, but I remembered how my father had been looking out there and thought better of it. I also remembered how I hadn't stuck up for Shane when Kevin McClendon made him eat that worm, and how Shane had looked at me afterward. Childhood embarrassment will stick with a person. I supposed I remember that day just as clearly as Shane, the shame of my inaction. I'd soon lose contact with Kevin McClendon, whose parents would give up their struggling pig operation and move them all nearer to the city. Just after high school, Shane Wilson would be killed when he drove his own father's pick-up into a telephone pole. No skid marks branded the pavement where the truck sped Shane to his death.

In addition to the house and barn and silo, we had two outbuildings on our land. One of those was full of machinery and other equipment, but the second was little more than a shed, empty save for a few random items: a cracked bucket, a wooden box missing its top, various rusted-out crank drills and hammers, and a cup of nails sitting on a counter-high work space. It stood only a hundred or so yards from our front porch, but had been in a state of ignored disuse for so long that it was barely seen, as though it wasn't even there. Like some browned-out shrub nobody had yet taken the time to rip up. I went there on bored afternoons to pretend it was a castle I had to protect, or the hideout of a thief I'd been tasked to apprehend. On this day it was to be a cabin far off on a winter mountaintop. But as I got close, I heard something from inside and peered through a break between the wall slats. The blinding sun was lowering on the other side of the shed, slicing through the small room in shards. My father stood in front of the work space with his back to me, his pants slung low enough for me to see the pale skin of his rear. Two bare legs wrapped around his waist. He made slight movements. Though his head and shoulders hid Estelle's face, I recognized the long red-blonde hair flung over his shoulder. She emitted a repeated noise, a faint *ha ha ha*. My father puffed short breaths through his nose, the same as when he chopped wood and hit the log clean.

I stepped silently backward a few yards, a safe distance. I was about to break into a run and hide behind a low berm on the other side of our driveway to wait until they came out. To see whatever I would see. I couldn't imagine. But before I got halfway there I saw my mother in the doorway of our house, the screen open. She was in a black and yellow dress, her hair down just the way it was each and every day. And, like always, she wore that look of exhaustion on her face, that expression I could never quite understand or forgive. She raised a hand and waved at me with her fingers. Without thinking, I checked on the shed to see if anything could be detected from where I stood. Then she looked over at it. If there was any surprise on her face, any burst of understanding, it disappeared before I could register it. The little building remained still. But she suddenly seemed a bit sadder. She drew her eyes back to me and slowly raised her hand again and went inside the house, letting the screen door bang shut.

My mind darted back to the shed. I understood what I had seen. I'd heard talk of it at school with friends, though the details of the act as reported (usually by boys with older brothers) were always fuzzy and, as often as not, doubtful. For all that mystery, it was amazing how clear it was at the moment of witness. And I understood my father wanting to be close to Estelle. Estelle laughed and Estelle smelled good. Estelle, as far as I could tell, didn't know the first thing about Tchaikovsky, or care. Sex was for married people, of course, for husbands and wives, but somehow my nine-year-old self also had the inkling of an understanding of adultery, an understanding beyond the definition. I understood why. I sympathized with my father and Estelle. I took their side. It was okay what they were doing, maybe even good.

—

When I came back to the house an hour later, my family was just sitting down at the table, along with Estelle and Robert. My mother was at the counter, cutting a chicken into pieces. "I was calling you," she said.

"There he is," Robert said. I hadn't seen or heard his truck coming down our drive. I felt like I hadn't seen him in days, though it had been only hours since my father chewed him out by the barn. His thin hair had been freshly combed back.

"Where have you been?" my father asked.

"I was at Shane Wilson's," I lied.

"Admiring his daddy's fields?"

"No," I said. "I don't know." His face was like it always was: round and reddish and stubbled.

"All right, well, sit down there." He tapped on the table in front of my seat. "Get some food in you."

"Smells delicious," Estelle said to my mother, who told her, "I'm glad."

Estelle smiled and there was a moment where her mouth hung open and it looked as if she was going to say something else. But she didn't. She went back to looking at her plate, straightening the napkin on her lap. Her hair was pulled neatly back in a ponytail. A small blotch of red showed on the skin over her collarbone. Small enough that no one would have questioned it. It was a hot day. Skin goes crazy.

I turned and found my father looking at me. His hands were folded beneath his chin and he eyes were squinted.

"How is that Wilson boy?" he said. "Scrawny little thing, isn't he?"

"I guess so," I said.

"What was it that other boy made him do, lick a turd or some such?"

"Eat a worm," I said. I glanced across the table at my sister, thinking about the conversation we'd had earlier, thinking about that little rock I threw and how it sent her away. But she was looking out the window, her mind somewhere else completely.

"That's terrible," my mother said, dishing food onto plates.

"That's boys," my father corrected her.

"That's good protein, too, I imagine," Robert joked.

"Maybe he should put more in his diet," my father said. "Get some muscle on his bones."

"He's just a child," my mother said.

"Must have dug deep to get a worm in these conditions," Robert said.

My father took a tug off a piece of bread. "Got them sprinklers," he said.

"Oh," Robert said, "that's right." As if just remembering that not every farm had the difficulties we did. Not every man was out tending to hard, dry dirt.

My mother served each of us before sitting down with her own small portion. Chicken and potatoes and peas. Even the peas tasted good. Everything my mother cooked tasted good. When she set my plate in front of me she paused to put her hand on my head. How was I to know then what it was to love a child, the way that love is like grief. She smoothed down my hair and then curled her fingers in, as if to take a little piece with her, to slide it into the pocket of her apron.

Our old lab, Petal, walked across the room in her slow, arthritic gait. She carefully leaned forward, stretching her front legs and raising her rear. Her tail went up, giving us a view of her backside.

"Don't you wink your bung at me," my father said. Harriet giggled and then said, "Eww." "Karl," my mother said. Petal looked back at us and let go a squeak of a fart. That sent us all into fits of laughter, even my mother, though she tried to hide it. I laughed harder and longer than anyone else, tearing up, giggling uncontrollably at that slow, gassy old dog.

"We're gonna have to be going right after dinner," Robert said after a minute. "O'Connor's staying open so I can pick up that brake drum, but I got to get there by six."

"What about ice cream?" Harriet said.

"What's this?" my mother said.

"Oh," Estelle said, "I mentioned maybe we'd go into town for some dessert. I hope that's okay."

"That's fine," my father said. "You go on over to O'Connor," he said to Robert, "and we'll get the kids their sweets, then you can meet us and be on your way." Robert looked at his wife, but Estelle just went about cutting and chewing her food. My father gestured at her with his fork. "She doesn't want to go over there. You kidding? O'Connor gets talking. Old man'll bore the woman to death."

"Yeah," Robert said after a moment. "I guess you're right."

"Don't suppose you want to come?" my father said to my mother.

"Maybe next time," she said. "Anyway, not too much room in that old truck of yours."

"Nothing wrong with that truck," he snapped.

"I didn't say there was, Karl."

"Yeah," he said. There was a pause during which none of us spoke or even looked up from our plates of food. There was just Petal clacking across the floor in the living room. Finally my father said, "Chicken's good," and took another bite.

—

A while after dinner we piled in, my father behind the wheel, then me, then Estelle with Harriet halfway on her lap. It was tight, but once we started, the wind through the windows cooled us and I liked being forced against my father's side.

We got into town and it was still hot and the ice-cream parlor was doing brisk business, the line to the counter a dozen people deep. As we waited I thought of how good this was, standing there with my father and Estelle, even with my sister. After a few minutes my father sighed and handed a dollar to Estelle. "We'll be outside," he told her. "Chocolate and chocolate," he said, pointing first to himself and then me. On the sidewalk, folks were heading to the pictures. My father set his hand on my shoulder and took me slowly against the general stream of people.

"Did I hear you threw a rock at your sister?" he said.

"I don't know," I said.

"Well, you can trust me that that's what I heard. Are you saying you don't know if you threw a rock at your sister or not?"

I said nothing.

"Listen to me here," he said. "You don't throw rocks at your sister. You know better than that." He took us to a bench. We sat down and he gestured vaguely back toward the ice-cream shop. "They'll see us over here," he said, and then continued. "Don't throw rocks at girls. There's a way men treat women. You need to protect them, son. Other people try to throw rocks, your job is to stop them. I know they can be a handful, but still that's no reason."

Something about this sounded crooked. I was old enough to recognize hypocrisy, even if I wouldn't for some more years be able to conjure the word. I knew the difference between practicing and preaching. I wondered then how he protected my mother. Or Estelle. But I still felt that if there had been a compact broken between my parents, surely it was my mother who rendered the first betrayal through her refusal to leave the house.

Estelle and Harriet joined us with our ice creams. We fit ourselves onto the bench and ate in silence. Robert showed up after we were finished and our father said, "All right, then," and the three of us got into the truck.

We took the long way, swinging a few blocks to the south before heading back up toward the farm. There were houses just off downtown, tall Victorians that people called the Painted Ladies. They were decorated with bright colors on the eaves and shutters and doors and window frames. Delicate woodwork spiraled and laced along wraparound porches. Each one was unique. Each one a testament to the early days of the century, when Sycamore and a thousand other towns like it were flush with money and spirit, established by men whose family names were known. They were built with precision and lived in with what I imagined was a kind of clean elegance. We stared as if we were looking at both the past and the future simultaneously, the what-was and the what-if. I indulged in fantasies of leisure and power. Servants. Underlings in vague business ventures. Cars in the drive. Sometimes a wife, though at the moment I hardly understood the use of one.

—

"This year we start home economics," Harriet said to our mother, who was sewing up a hole in one of my father's shirts. The three of us were in the living room and I was curled into the wingback, picking at the stiff metal links of an old horse bit. "And they're having all the mothers come in. A different girl's mother each week to help out with the class."

Our mother did not look up from her stitching. "That right?" she said. Then, "Where is your father?"

"Checking on Gracie," I said. He'd been gone for a while by then. He hadn't even come in after we got back from town.

"I told Mrs. Samuels about what a good cook you are," Harriet said, "and she told me there'd be plenty of weeks we'd be doing cooking and baking. She said all the mothers would be choosing whatever they wanted to do. If they want to make a pie or cook up a casserole or, well, anything." She drummed her hands on the book in her lap. "Anything else, either," she went on. "It doesn't even have to be cooking. If you want to show the girls about that stitching or just keeping house, I'm sure that would be fine."

"Well," our mother said, and then paused. "Well, let's talk about that closer to schooltime."

"You could probably show everyone a thing or two about doing up a chicken," Harriet said, smiling.

Our mother nodded. "I'll keep that in mind." She bit off the line of the thread she'd been working into the shirt and tugged at the fabric, testing the strength of the stitches. Then she picked up a pair of jeans and went about re-threading her needle.

My sister left it at that and said she was tired. She kissed our mother good night and went to her room.

In the silence between my mother and me there hung information. Information I had, and information she had. And there was some we shared, but neither of us was quite sure what exactly that was.

"I guess it's about your bedtime, too," she said.

"Maybe she should bring Estelle to school with her," I said.

She finally looked up from her stitching. "Say that again?"

I tried to make it sound casual. Something that just made simple sense. But my face was hot. "Maybe Harri should bring Estelle with her to her class."

"Why would you say that?"

I shrugged. The smell of chicken remained in the air, warm and salty. I felt sick in my stomach. The radio was dead quiet in the corner. My mother kept her green eyes on me, waiting for me to say what she hoped I couldn't. "I looked over in the shed today," I said.

Her cheeks dropped. "I think it's time you head on to bed."

"I was gonna go in there and play—"

"Head on up to bed now."

"It was strange—"

"That's *enough*," she said sternly.

I held her gaze for a moment and then got up and went to the front door, pushed open the screen, and stepped onto our porch, letting the door thwack closed behind me. There were a million things I could not have known right then. I did not know, for instance, that we would survive the dry season that year, barely, and that my father would continue to eke out something like a living for years to come. I did not know that in three years my mother would be gone, having finally escaped the house by way of a rope and a sturdy beam. Harriet would be the one to find her and be the first to sprinkle black dirt onto her casket amidst the old stones of Lily Lake cemetery. I did not know that Harriet would leave us, too, as soon as she could, off to college just after her eighteenth birthday, and later to her own family and life. Or that Robert would one day buy his own parcel of land, that our interactions with him and Estelle would be reserved to moments in town when my father refused to talk to either of them. And I could not see to the time when my father would pass and the farm would be sold off to real estate developers who would raze each building, starting with that shed, and tear out the crop without harvesting so much as a kernel. These events would come in their own time, but each and all of them are now wrapped up, inextricable, in what had just transpired between my mother and me.

My father sat on the porch swing. After a moment, music from the radio came on inside. Softly. My breathing became heavy and my body tense. I had to keep from crying. I wanted to scream and to put my small fists into my father's chest, his red face, but I stood motionless just outside the door, paralyzed with knowledge. The air was still hot. There were no clouds in the sky. He tipped his hat back off his forehead and kept his eyes out on the hard fields.

"This goddamn season," he said.

The Ridiculous Future

I was in the kitchen making dinner when my son came in and asked if I'd seen the new neighbors. "They're out there with a truck," Steven said. It had only been a few days since we realized that the Indian family across the hall had left. I lowered the volume on the stereo where Floyd was singing about money on the record player. This was 1986, but *Dark Side* was still the best album around as far as I was concerned, hands down.

"They look weird," Steven continued.

"Explain," I said.

"Like weirdoes," he said.

I went to the sliding balcony door and pushed apart the hanging blinds. The sun was falling away, turning itself orange and the rest of the sky purple. Three floors below in the parking lot, two men were carrying a wooden armoire down the metal ramp of a U-Haul. Both of them wore black T-shirts, but from the distance I couldn't tell anything more except that they were thin. And young, I guessed. Younger than me, anyway.

"What's so weird about them?" I asked Steven.

He came to the door and looked down. "You can't tell from here," he said.

The men were almost to the end of the ramp when the armoire came apart as if sawed in half by an invisible blade, the top and bottom falling and crashing into the metal.

I slid the door open and stepped out. "You need some help?" I called. The two of them looked up and found me on the balcony.

"Dad," Steven said anxiously.

I called down, "Get that stuff aside and we'll see what we can do with some wood glue and finishing nails." It wasn't like me to do. I suppose I was feeling especially lonely.

Steven followed me downstairs and then I could see what he was saying. The one had spiked black hair and the other's was kind of blond and pink at the same time. They looked like they were from MTV. I kneeled down where they had placed the broken pieces of the armoire. "Let's take a look at this," I said, and then "I'm David."

"Kyle," the leader said. "That's Burt." Pink-hair flashed a crooked smile.

"This is my son, Steven," I said, forgetting that he told me he didn't like being introduced that way. It embarrassed him, he had told me once, which pissed me off a little at the time.

Kyle said, "What's up," and then gave Steven a little wave without taking his thumb out of his jeans pocket.

"It's not even really worth it," Kyle said. "Thing's a piece of shit."

"It's not bad," I said. "You put it together yourself?"

"My wife did."

I looked up at him for a second and then got my eyes back to the thing. "She have some parts left over?" I said, kidding around.

Kyle thought about this for a second and then said, "I don't even know, dude."

I added a few extra nails to keep it sturdy, and then helped bring it upstairs. Steven took a crate of records and looked to be struggling, but said he was fine in that annoyed voice he uses when I'm cramping his style. The apartment looked pretty much the same as ours, the same layout. We had some decent furniture, a matching wood buffet and china cabinet, a comfortable couch—artifacts left over from the old house—and that helped to mask the place. Seeing this one, though, was a cold reminder of the day we moved in. The carpet in Kyle's place was the same stained tan as ours, the walls the same faded eggshell. There was a hole in the wall by the door that matched the one in our bathroom that I'd been on maintenance to fix since we moved in. This was the slums of the suburbs we lived in, a collection of hulking shit-brown buildings, half the units Section 8. The kind of place I still felt I had to explain.

"We're across the hall," I said after helping with a couple more loads of boxes.

"You'll have to meet my wife soon," Kyle said.

I opened the door and gave a wave of my hand to Kyle's friend. As I turned, Steven gave a quick nod to the room and said, "Gentlemen."

Kyle let out a quick breath of a laugh and said, "See you, man."

We got into our apartment I said to Steven, "Gentlemen?" He smiled the big toothy grin that he got from Caroline and then pressed the power button on the remote.

I don't know why it surprised me so much to hear Kyle say he had a wife that first night. Caroline and I were young when we got married—I was twenty, she nineteen—and we had Steven pretty soon after that. I'm thirty-two and most people my age—at least the few I know—are just starting families now, or just getting around to even thinking about it. And here I am with a twelve-year-old. Not that I would change it. I wouldn't. That kid knocks me out daily. He is seriously smart, smarter than I'll ever be. During the period after his mother's death he still did every bit of homework his friend brought him from school. The principal called me to express his condolences and all that and to make sure we knew that Steven would get a pass on assignments for a couple weeks. When I told this to Steven, he said that he knew already, and then he went back to his schoolbook. The funeral was the next morning and he still made sure to know all about Betsy Ross.

—

One day school let out and I was just coming outside and someone shouted, "Steven!" and I looked up and out past the fence was Kyle. I had seen him around the complex a few times since they moved in and my dad helped him with his cabinet. I'd be sitting on the front step and he'd come up and ask me how my day was and tell me about when he went to school in the city, how he used to cut class and take the train and bum around record stores and the parking lot of a Dunkin' Donuts. Every time we talked I wondered if he was just being nice, hanging out with the lonely kid. None of my friends lived in our complex. But every time he would keep the conversation going, asking me questions, and I would tell him about school and a little about my old school and neighborhood, tell stories about my old friends, and he would listen closely, like he was trying to understand exactly who I was.

Now, his friend Burt stood off to the side. Between them was a girl. I guess I knew she was probably Erin. I know I hoped she was, anyway. She was short and thin, with blonde hair, long, pulled back into a ponytail with the sides and back of her head shaved. Kyle pointed down the street to where a white limousine was waiting at a red light and said, "I got our ride, man. Living the dream!" The limo pulled away.

"Who are they?" this kid Randall asked.

"My neighbors."

"Figures," another kid, this kid Jerry, said and I knew it was about where we lived. I guess I was friends with these other boys—I was invited to their houses for sleepovers and birthdays—but it seemed like they all knew each other since they were born. I was the new kid and most of the time it felt like I always would be.

"Come walk with us," Kyle called.

Burt said, "Let's go, dude."

I left the schoolyard and joined my punk rock neighbors, feeling great walking out the gate with Kyle slapping me on the back.

"This is Erin," he said.

Her skin was white like paper. She had blue eyes just like Kyle, but hers were big. His were smaller and stuck back in his face. My eyes are brown, and they aren't big or little, just regular. She shook my hand and said, "You're, like, Kyle's favorite person."

"Burt got a bootleg of *Suburbia*," Kyle said.

"Check it out," Burt said and handed me a black unmarked VHS tape.

"It's a classic, man," Kyle said.

Near the entrance to the apartment complex, a group of Hispanic guys were working on the engine of a Buick. They yelled something in Spanish and laughed.

"Is your dad on the dole or something?" Burt said to me. Erin told him to shut up. "I'm just wondering why they live here," he said.

Kyle said, "Don't listen to him."

I didn't know what the dole was.

The movie we watched was about a bunch of punk rockers living together. They go to concerts and jump around to the music and have sex and one of them dies from drugs. It wasn't anything like regular movies. All the actors were terrible. But Kyle and Erin and Burt seemed to really like it, and I could see why. It was all about them.

Kyle was outside school at least a couple times a week. It was on his way home from his job at the Jewel-Osco, but I also think now that he timed it right so that we could walk together. And if my dad was working the evening shift I would hang out in their apartment and they would play music and tell me about the bands or we'd watch TV or sit on the balcony if it was nice. Burt was there most of the time. He never smiled unless he was being sarcastic. But Erin smiled a lot and it seemed like Kyle was always laughing because of a joke I told or because he farted on me or because he was just looking around and thought everything was hilarious. Mostly when we hung out, they did the talking. I was happy just to listen.

I was having a hard time in history class around then. We were learning about the Holocaust and Mr. Slattery showed us slides of victims in the concentration camps and we watched a black-and-white movie about it all. For homework we read parts of the diary Anne Frank wrote before someone ratted her out. She died in one of the camps.

"She was just a kid," I said.

"That's right," Mr. Slattery said. "And what year did she go into hiding?" He was a short and wide man with blond hair. He was also the wrestling coach.

I said, "Nineteen forty-two."

And Mr. Slattery said, "And what year was she sent to the concentration camp?"

"Nineteen-forty-four," I said. I raised my hand and Mr. Slattery looked down, let out a breath, and said, "Yeah?"

"I still don't—" I started, but then I began to cry. Not a lot, but enough to stop the words from coming out of my mouth. The other kids looked at me, some laughing into the palms of their hands.

Mr. Slattery walked up to my desk with the hall pass, a piece of wood painted red, with the words in blue. "Go on to the bathroom, Steven. Take a minute and then come back ready to go over the reading."

It seemed like everyone else's brains were figuring out something that mine wasn't. It seemed like I was learning a million things, but I wanted to know something else. Like what good was us knowing all this to Anne Frank? Or to her dad who lost his whole family? Maybe it's like a puzzle and I just need to fill in all the pieces and then it'll make sense. But I doubt it.

—

On Parent-Teacher night I got to meet all those other adults Steven spends time with. Most of them were fine—bored and underpaid, but with moments of genuine enthusiasm. The other parents were all older than me. This is something I'd been dealing with since Steven was born. The question— *How* old is your kid?—and then the looks of surprise and curiosity, sometimes pity, often judgment. By the time we moved out of the old neighborhood everyone knew us and it wasn't an issue anymore, but now I had to endure it all again.

The history classroom was outfitted with maps and pictures of presidents and timelines running the length of the walls. Steven's teacher, Mr. Slattery, gave a short talk about the importance of understanding the past and not repeating it. The usual rigamarole. Afterwards we got a chance to talk with him one-on-one.

"Steven's a good kid," he said and I agreed. "A little sensitive, though."

"How do you mean?"

"Just, sensitive." He rolled his eyes back and waved his hands in small, flighty motions.

"I'm not sure what that means." I flopped my hands about. Slattery was about my age and he had a round face and red cheeks and thin blond hair. He looked like the kid from Family fucking Circus.

"Well, I don't know if he told you about the incident a couple weeks ago."

I told him I didn't think so and he smiled and said, "I'm not surprised." Then he told me about Steven crying in class. "He's just going to have to toughen up. That's all I'm saying. Again, a good kid."

Was this guy shitting me? "Let me get this straight," I said, a bit louder than I meant to. Some of the other parents looked over. "My boy is upset by the Holocaust and you think this is cause for concern. Shouldn't we be more concerned about kids who *aren't* upset by the Holocaust?"

"That's not exactly what I meant."

"Try it again." But he didn't. The bell rang and it was time for us to move on to the next room, the next teacher.

This was a Friday and Steven was staying at an overnight birthday party for a friend. Soon after I got home to the dark and silence of our apartment, there was a knock at the door. No one ever came over, except occasionally one of Steven's friends, but they had to call up to be buzzed through the security door. I looked through the fish-eyed peekhole and there was a pale blonde girl. She leaned into the door and opened her mouth towards my eye. I opened up.

"The carpenter himself," she said.

"David," I said.

"Erin." She put out a tiny, soft-skinned hand.

"You're the wife," I said. Somehow, though I'd seen Kyle and his ever-present friend around, I'd managed to not cross paths with Erin until now.

"I am the wife," she said. "I've been meaning to introduce

myself. And I wanted to thank you for fixing the cabinet. That was cool of you."

"Armoire," I corrected, and I immediately felt like a stickler, like a teacher.

"Yeah, the *ah-mooaah*." Her mouth opened like the end of an exaggerated kiss. "It's good to know there are good people around here."

"Well," I said, "yeah, we're okay."

"Don't sell yourself short, David. That was a right neighborly thing to do." She put a fist into my stomach, which I tensed too late. "Anyway, we were wondering if you wanted to hang out. We're just fucking around, listening to music. Drinking drinks."

I thought about the empty rooms behind me. I thought about falling asleep in front of *Friday Night Videos*. And I was happy to be looking at this girl's face. Her cheeks were full and round. Her hair was pulled up into a bouquet at the top of her head, revealing the short-shorn sides and back. Her cut-offs grabbed at her hips. I thought of how she must see me. The 14-hour black stubble. The square haircut parted on the side. The button-down shirt for a buttoned-down old man.

"Yeah," I said. "Should I bring anything?"

"Like what?" she asked. I didn't know. Then I remembered a going-away gift from a Greek guy at the mortgage company.

"I think I have a bottle of ouzo," I said.

"Hell yeah, bring that. We'll fuck it up."

I got the bottle and followed Erin's tiny frame the few steps across the hall. Though it had been a good month since they moved in, the apartment looked much the same. They had put up some posters and there were a couple lamps set on the floor, but the boxes that Steven and I helped with were still in the corner. The armoire I assumed was in the bedroom. On the white paint of the far wall, above where our dinette table across the hall would have been, someone had markered in loopy script words: *We are the ridiculous future.*

I couldn't help but think about their security deposit.

Kyle stood politely, somewhat nervously, when I came in. "Awesome," he said. "It's awesome that you're hanging out." He introduced some people whose names I instantly forgot. A few were on the ratty old couch that sat not quite flush with the wall, but mostly they were on the floor, sitting or lying, or somewhere in between. We sat on the floor and I presented the bottle. "Oh, wow," he said. "This looks expensive."

"I doubt it," I said.

He twisted the cap and tilted the top towards me. "You want the first pull?"

I almost said that I had glasses across the hall that I could bring over, but some of the people in the room were already looking at me like I worked for the government. "Sure," I said, and I took a good-sized swig. The liquorice taste coated my mouth and throat. I handed the bottle back and Kyle drank. He covered his mouth and said, "Oh, man."

"Let's try some of that over here," Burt said.

"Oh, man," Kyle said again and passed the bottle.

Everyone was talking, yelling about people I didn't know, this or that band, putting on records until someone else took it off and replaced it with something else. Then more arguing. I didn't particularly like the music, but at the time it seemed to communicate something about how I was feeling: angry with that Slattery son of a bitch, but happy with the company, happy to be awake and alive. At one point the music scratched to silence and Burt said, "This is for the old man," and he put on Bowie's *Ziggy* album. He cranked "Suffragette City" and they all did the "Hey man" part and yelled together any of the words they knew.

I asked Erin and Kyle what was their story and they told me. Kyle dropped out of high school his junior year and started working at a grocery store full time. When Erin graduated and turned eighteen they decided to get married, got the license and made an appointment at the courthouse without anyone knowing. Then they told their parents.

"My dad came," Kyle said, "but that was it."

"Your folks didn't come?" I asked Erin.

"They weren't happy about it," she said and took a sip of beer. "They want me in college. And I'm going to. I just don't see why I can't do both."

"You're going to college for sure," Kyle said happily. He turned to me. "This girl's smart as shit."

Erin scrunched up the side of her mouth and rolled her eyes.

I got pretty crocked on the ouzo and whatever beer they had in the fridge. There was plenty of it. I remembered having this same attitude when I was younger: quantity over quality. Caroline and I could tie one on. That's how Steven happened. Feeling good late one night, we couldn't get each other's clothes off fast enough. No protection. No thoughts of tomorrow.

I told Kyle and Erin about my meeting with Slattery.

"God, I knew teachers like that," Erin said.

"That's awesome that he cried," Kyle said. "That kid's the best. I wish he was here now."

"Well," I said. I certainly didn't want him there. I love him, but there's relaxing with your kid and there's relaxing with other adults, and these two were as close as I had to that right then.

It was nearly three when I left. They tried to get me to stay, but I couldn't keep awake any longer. Erin hugged me at the door. I let her go much sooner than I wanted to. And then Kyle came and put his arms around me. He was thin, but muscular. His arms went under mine, a childish hug.

That night in bed, in my fantasies, I was with Erin. I thought of her lips, her eyes and ears, her hair, her hands, her ass. I imagined kissing her chest—not just her breasts, but that inexplicably vast area below the base of her throat. That field of skin. There is so much to women.

—

I was walking home from school with Kyle one day and he said, "Hey, don't listen to that history teacher dick."

It felt like my stomach was empty all of a sudden. "Who told you something?" I said.

"Your dad," Kyle said. "That Holocaust shit is fucked up. Anyone who doesn't cry a little is a Nazi."

"I didn't cry," I said.

"It's no big deal," Kyle said.

"I know, but I didn't."

"Oh," he said. "Okay. Whatever then."

"Yeah," I said. "Whatever."

I was never so mad at my dad. It scared me, but I couldn't help it. He came home from work that night and said, "What's going on, bud?" I said, "Nothing," in a way that let him know I was angry.

"You doing homework?"

"Looks like it," I said, not taking my eyes off the textbook in front of me.

He waited a second. "What's with the attitude?"

"Why did you tell them about what happened in history?" I shouted. I motioned to the door, the hall, Kyle and Erin's apartment. My dad ran his hand over his forehead, but didn't say anything. I said to him, "I didn't even know you knew and now everybody knows?"

He looked around the room. "Come on, they don't care."

"I don't care if they care!" I yelled.

"Look, it just came out. We were sitting there talking and it just came out. If it embarrassed you, I'm sorry."

"Where were you?" It didn't make any sense why they would be sitting anywhere with my dad.

"We were just listening to music."

"At their house?" I asked.

"Yes, Steven, at their house. Why does it matter?"

"Because they're my friends!"

Over the next few days, I was determined to stay angry. It wasn't easy and I had to keep reminding myself. I avoided Kyle and Erin. I went up the stairs fast each day and I didn't leave the apartment if I didn't have to. I didn't know if they noticed. I hoped so. I imagined them talking about me. *Where has Steven been*? I imagined Kyle some night waking Erin up to say that he was worried. *Where is he anyway*?

—

I spent time at the neighbors' on nights that Steven was out with his friends. A couple of times I went over after he'd fallen asleep. Sometimes there was pot, once or twice coke. I only did a little. Most of the time it was just a whole lot of beer. I started bringing some over, to contribute. Always there was music, some of which I came to enjoy. Their friends would give me a hard time, asking if I wanted to jump across the hall and get some Steely Dan. Often we ended up dancing. Sometimes it would happen naturally, but more often than not, early or late in the night when I said I had to go—Steven would be home soon or I had to get up in the morning—Kyle would put on Bowie or the Buzzcocks and we would bob to the drums until we found our movements.

Finally, after some weeks of becoming whatever we were becoming, Kyle asked me about Steven, about his mother. We were standing in the kitchen. There were five or six kids lounging around the living room. Erin came and stood with us. I told the two of them the story, the version I have for moments like these. The wedding downtown, the pregnancy, Steven's birth, the house, the cancer. I stopped there, skipping the parts about my mini-breakdown, about losing my job, losing our home, and moving here to the complex. They could imagine those parts. And if they couldn't, lucky them.

"That's rough, man," Kyle said, patting me on the shoulder.

I cracked open another beer even though I was already pretty gone.

"I can't believe he had to go though that," Kyle said. It took me a second to realize that he meant Steven.

"Dude," someone yelled from the living room, "there's about to be a fight out there." Kyle rushed over to where his friends were looking out the glass door. Erin and I slowly followed. In the parking lot two groups of men were facing off. Each of them had one man out front, generals leaning in close.

"I'm going," Burt said.

"You coming?" Kyle said either to me or Erin, or both.

"Please," Erin said dismissively.

I told him no. I was too old for that.

"Let's go," Burt said. He was already in the hall.

The guys left and Erin went back to the kitchen to get another drink. "Idiots," she said.

This was the first time I'd been alone with her since we met in the doorway. Now I knew her, and now I was drunk and feeling as lonely as I ever had. I followed her and when she turned I leaned down and kissed her on the mouth. I had thought of nothing past this moment. She could have hit me. She could have hit me and then run out and told Kyle. He and his friends, all jacked up from the fight outside, surely would have hurt me. She could have shaken her head slowly, quietly told me to go home. She didn't. After a second I felt her tongue touching mine, timidly at first, then with some force. She put her hands on my hips. My hand slid down her back. The other held the side of her head where her hair was shaved. I moved my mouth to her neck and she passed her hand over the front of my pants.

"Fuck," she whispered, and then she pulled away. She went to the door and locked it.

"What if they come back up?"

"I'll say I didn't want cops busting in because of the fight. We got dope and shit all over the place." She came back and I kissed her again. Her breath was warm and beery and metallic. She took my head in her hands. We had so little time. I wanted more. Not minutes, but hours. Not days, but months. Not a decade, but lifetimes.

"Okay," she said, moving her mouth from mine. "Here." She moved my body so that I was facing the sink and then she unzipped my pants and scooted herself onto the edge of the counter. "You gotta be fast, though."

I was. As I climaxed my hand moved across her shoulder and gripped the collar of her V-neck, the backs of my fingers pressed against the cool skin just below the base of her throat.

—

Every night my dad would say, "How was your today?" and I would answer him with a shrug.

"Well," he would say. He made dinner and we ate, but I didn't say much to him.

One night, he was in his room reading the paper and I was watching TV. When the show went to commercial, in the silence before the commercial started, I heard yelling through the front door. I turned down the volume and listened. A man's voice, then a woman's. Kyle and Erin. I went and leaned into the door and turned my head to hear better. I only made out a few words, "no," and "you," and a lot of cursing. My dad came out.

"What's going on?"

I didn't look at him, but kept my ear pressed against the door. "I don't know," I whispered.

He came to the door and stood behind me. I looked back and he had his head just like mine. Their voices became a little more clear, like my dad and I both listening doubled the volume. Erin said, "They're just saying that…" Kyle said, "…why you're even listening to them…" Kyle yelled, "I'm your family now!"

We listened until the fighting stopped. And then we still stood there for a while even though there was nothing to hear but the high pitch of the silent TV.

We heard more yelling almost every night. My dad and I had made up or I just stopped being mad, and we would be watching TV or having a bucket of chicken when the voices came again. My dad would turn up the volume and we would pretend like it wasn't there. I hated it, but it seemed to bother my dad even more. His body would tense up. His leg would bounce and I knew he wasn't really watching whatever we were watching. A door would slam and he'd jump in his seat and say to himself, "Jesus."

At school, Mr. Slattery started giving us more quizzes and tests, mostly matching the event to the date, the capital to the country, the general to the war. Even though everyone in the room was doing it, I always felt singled out, like he was trying to prove something to me.

—

It happened twice more, Erin and I. A couple weeks later she came by when I had a weekday off and Steven was at school.

She stood in the doorway same as she had the first time I saw her. We chatted about nothing for a bit and then I reached a hand and put it to her hip and she leaned into it and then into me and I closed the door behind her. The light was white coming into my bedroom and it reflected wildly off her skin. Next to Erin's lithe frame I felt conscious of how thick I'd become around my middle and how dark my arm and chest hair had become. I kept hearing that song by The Police about the teacher and student. But if guilt about our ages or her marriage or Caroline or Steven was making a chase after me, it quickly fell behind and I ran on. Erin was the first woman in my bedroom in the apartment. I'd slept with a couple in the years since Caroline died, none more than twice. And none had I brought home. It was thrilling to have her there, to feel her under me, surrounded by all the ordinary objects of my life. It seemed incredible that she could open her eyes and see my alarm clock, even the radio station I had it tuned to, that she could witness my laundry pile, my penny jar, the Tribune from the weekend before. The smells of my home and belongings mixed with the scent of her hair.

After, she said, "This doesn't have anything to do with Kyle. You know?"

"I think so."

"I'm just saying, we're all adults, right?"

"Absolutely."

She got dressed and said, "So, I'll see you."   The next time was in the bathroom of their apartment. Kyle and Burt went for a beer run. It was quick and not at all what you might call romantic, but what it lacked in those trappings of a love affair it made up for with illicitness. The dangers of what we were doing were suddenly not to be pushed out of my mind, but embraced. We could be discovered—it made my heart race. And she was a different person. It was a bit like our time in the kitchen, but she was even more in control. As soon as the boys left she was on me, aiming her mouth vaguely for mine but not caring if she missed completely. I remember I had a jean jacket on and she took me by the collar into the john. She was wearing the same skirt she wore our first time, a little black number with these metal rivet things running along the hem, and I wondered if she wore it on purpose. Maybe she set the whole thing up: stocked just enough beer, invited just me and Burt, knowing that Kyle would want company and be fine with leaving her alone with me. Maybe, but who cared. My back was on the cold tile of the floor and she gripped down on my shoulders tight with her hands like she wanted to tear me in two. When we were done she sat on the toilet and peed and I cleaned myself up with tissue. We hitched up our underwear and that was it, our last time. Not that I knew it at the time. No, right then I wanted to keep going for however long we could.

"Better do something about that grin," she said.

—

On Halloween some of the other boys and I went out walking through the neighborhoods around our school. We weren't trick-or-treating, just being out with all the kids in their costumes. It was pretty cold that night and wet. We kicked sticks and soggy leaves from the wet sidewalk. It was that time between day and night, that time that my dad sometimes calls the magic hour. We could all still see each others' faces, but soon we wouldn't.

Randall and Jerry had bags full of shaving cream and toilet paper and some other stuff that they had snagged from their kitchens and bathrooms or that their older brothers bought for them. We were waiting until full dark. I wasn't too crazy about the idea, even though I knew it would pretty much wash right off. Our complex would get bombed at least once a month and it would be there for a few days and then just disappear. But still it made me nervous. Then Randall said that we should go over to Slattery's house. Randall was on the wrestling team and Slattery had them over for pizza at the end of the season the last year.

"He lives right over there," Randall said, pointing down a street that was getting darker by the second.

Slattery had been talking for weeks about how he and his wife were going up to his cabin in Wisconsin for the weekend. He always talked differently when he talked about his cabin, like this kid Kevin when he first moved here after his family sold their farm in Kentucky. "How many acres do you think I got up there?" Slattery asked us one day, right in the middle of our quiet reading period. "Sixteen," he said. "Sixteen pretty little acres." He even brought in pictures one day and showed them to us. The place looked okay, I guess, and I probably would have liked it if it was ours, but I didn't think it was so great that I'd be bragging about it all the time.

All the princesses and Michael Jacksons and hippies and ghosts were heading back home with their parents and the streets were pretty much empty. Randall took us to Slattery's house, which was dark inside. I recognized his little tan hatchback in the driveway. Everybody was shushing everybody and a couple of the guys didn't hesitate before chucking rolls of toilet paper up in the trees in his front yard. Randall and Jerry were tossing us the stuff out of their bags. I caught a bar of soap.

"What is this for?" I whispered.

"The windows," Jerry said. He pointed at the car. "You write with it."

"What do I write?" I said, but he was gone, flinging spurts of shaving cream across the lawn.

I walked to the back of the car and looked at the big, wide window. My mind was as blank as that glass. If I was on one of the sports teams I could have written Go Cougars or something like that. If I was a different sort of kid I would have scratched out the F-word. I thought about Slattery's class, but nothing funny came into my head. All I could think of was those tests and all those facts he wanted us to remember. So I wrote one of those. 1492. The year Columbus landed in America. I knew it was stupid and that the guys would probably just scrunch their eyes and think to themselves of a hundred better things they would have written, but it felt like what I wanted to say. I wrote another, 1776—the year of the Declaration of Independence—and another, 1783—when British troops left the colonies. I wrote 1942 and 1944 because I was still thinking about Anne Frank a lot. I wrote 1969 for the moon landing and 1972 for Watergate. I jumped back to 1865 for the end of the Civil War and then back more to 1812 for the beginning of that one. I was going fast and probably no one would be able to read them, but I thought of more. 1917. 1849. I scribbled George Washington and Paul Revere and Little Big Horn. Then that led me to Trail of Tears, which took up a whole side window. Pearl Harbor got another side. The glass was almost covered and I was regretting writing some of the words so big. I suddenly had a lot to say. I fit JFK into the crook of a seven, and in a corner below that Cuba Missile. I wrote Ho Chi Minh and started to feel weird about everything being about war and stuff, so I wrote MTV on the passenger side mirror and Punk on the driver's.

Then the guys were saying, "Come on, come on," and I turned around to see Slattery's trees covered with toilet paper and his lawns dotted with white cream. They chucked the cans into his bushes and so I tossed in the soap. None of the guys looked at what I had written. We all started just running down the street, happy and terrified. I wondered if Kyle would have thought it was hilarious or just stupid, what we'd done. I figured he'd think it was great and I ran faster and made it almost all the way home before stopping to catch my breath.

—

I saw less of both Erin and Kyle. The gatherings at their place stopped and I would only occasionally pass them in the on the stairs, when, if they were together, Kyle would nod vaguely and Erin would avoid eye contact. Once or twice, I saw Erin by herself and she would put an all too brief hand on my arm and move on. They both seemed incredibly and suddenly overwhelmed. Steven and I had been hearing them fight, more and more, for weeks. Their arguing made its way across the hall, through the flimsy walls. Of course, I was convinced he knew something about us. Each night, whether we heard them or not, I waited for the pounding on the door. I couldn't blame him. I'd been married and I knew what I would have wanted to do if I'd been made a cuckold. Kyle should have torn me apart. In my daily visions of the incident, I took the beating I had coming. I only wondered if Steven would be there to see it. This was my great fear. A boy will remember that sort of thing for a good long time.

But it didn't come. After a while, the fighting stopped. So did the music and the television. My affair with Erin ended, too. Nothing was said, but the time passed, days and then weeks, and it was the sort of thing you simply know. The air is different. The nights in our place seemed endless. I spent too much time smoking cigarettes on our balcony, thinking about my times with Erin. I worried about her in a way I couldn't quite define. I knew Kyle would never hurt her, so it wasn't that. I suppose I simply worried about her future, about all her potential. There are too many things that can happen in a life to throw you off your course. The bitch of it is that you can never really see it all until it's in the rearview.

—

The weather was cold by the time I finally knocked on their

door. It was a Saturday morning, around ten. My dad was still asleep back in our house. I heard movement from inside Kyle and Erin's and so stayed there in the hall, but it took a while for the latches to be undone. Kyle peered around the door. He looked like he hadn't slept. His hair was greasy and down over his forehead. His skin looked gray.

"Hey man," he said, quiet but happy. "Where've you been?"

"Here, I guess."

"Shit," he mumbled, "hang on a second." He closed the door and even though it was only a minute, I couldn't help thinking that he was playing some joke—let's see how long the kid will stay there—but then it opened again. "Come in," he said.

"How've you been?" he asked, rumpling my hair. I sat on the couch. He pulled on a pair of pants from the floor by the couch.

"Okay," I said. The floor and tables were covered in beer cans and ash trays and bottles.

He made his way slowly to the kitchen. "Water?" he asked while filling a glass. I said no, thanks. He came back, sat down on the couch with me, looked at me for a good long few seconds. He breathed and said, "You wanna do something today?"

"Like what?" I asked.

"I don't know," he said. "What should we do? It's Saturday, right. Let's go do something."

He said to hang on and went to the bedroom door, the one that would have been my dad's if we were at our place. He leaned into the room. "I'm going out," he said into the room. I heard Erin say, "What?" She sounded asleep still. Kyle shut the door. In the bedroom Erin raised her voice. "Kyle, what?"

"Let's go," Kyle said to me.

We got into his car and he cranked the heat. It came out

cold at first, but after we started moving it warmed.

"We're going to this place," he said. "It's cold. You got double socks?"

"No," I said.

"Long johns?"

"No."

"Alright, well, fuck it, me neither."

I didn't ask where we were going. I didn't want to. We drove north up busy streets until the road went from four lanes to two. The convenient stores and strip malls went away. The street light posts turned to trees. Kyle opened his window a sliver and leaned so that the air messed with his hair.

The further north we went the more I started to feel anxious. My stomach turned as we passed side streets: Grant, Hoover, Illinois. Little cul-de-sacs of big houses. I wondered again if he was playing some trick on me, some game. We passed Edison Middle School and I saw the soccer field, the basketball court and the track around it. I saw the jungle gym, left over from when it was still an elementary school. I cut my knee open there, I could have told him. There, when we were messing around at recess. I had to go to the hospital and get five stitches. My mom came in crying. I still have the scar.

I could have been directing him with my thoughts. He took a left on Rand, a right on Algonquin, into the entrance for the Nature Preserve. We parked near the Welcome Building and Kyle got out and said, "This is my favorite place." He made for the nearest trail into the woods and said, "This way."

"No, here," I said, and went for the trail up the road and on the left.

Kyle followed and we smiled as we made our way. This was the quiet trail. Here, there was just the sound of our feet on the dirt and leaves. The woodchucks running back and forth. Squirrels battling over walnuts. It was called the Muir Loop, I told Kyle. "It was named after a famous guy named

John Muir," I said.

"I think I've heard of him," Kyle said, but he didn't seem too sure about it.

"He founded the Sierra Club."

I remembered it perfectly. This first part of the trail was wide and graveled. The elms hung over the trail, like fingers above us. But then the trail splits and the one I led us down was narrower and the trees above us were almost solid and we could hardly see the sky past them. We walked through the leaves and over the roots that popped up on the trail. This trail wasn't kept neat like the others. This trail was a trail only because of the feet that stomped the ground to dirt and the legs that snapped the little low branches that tried to get in the way.

We came to an opening where there was a big pond with lily pads floating on the top. "I always go the other way," Kyle said.

"This way is better."

"No kidding."

We plunked down on the ground and stayed there for at least an hour. Every once in a while, some small, pointy thing would land on one of the pads and snag bugs off the surface. I told him the names that I knew.

"Look, look," I said. Coming in low on the far side of the pond was a Great Egret. It was long and stark white and perfect.

"Oh, shit," Kyle said so quietly I could barely hear him.

When I was little and came here with my mom, she told me stories about the birds when we weren't around. When we weren't looking, she said, the birds would play games in the trees, daring each other to walk out to the thinnest branches. They would tempt each other with big worms they had dug up. And when one would take the challenge, the others would squawk and chirp and flap their wings—this was them laughing. The one on the drooping branch would hop as soft as he could further and further. He knew this was a game and if he lost his balance or the branch broke, he could fly and keep away from the hard ground, but the fun part was being up on the branch, pretending he didn't have wings.

Kyle tucked his hand into his armpits. All he had was a jean jacket. "Do you want to go?" I asked him. He didn't look at me, just kept staring at the pond.

"If you want to," he said.

But we didn't. We stayed longer, watching the birds and the trees and the reflections of it all in the water.

—

I held on to my job at a mortgage company for a couple years after Caroline died. I wasn't surprised when they let me go: I was what you might call a highly distracted employee. Really, I just couldn't do it anymore, looking through pages and pages of people's lives, deciding whether or not they deserved a home. Of course, soon after we had to give up our home, so there's your irony. I took an assistant manager position at a furniture store, but couldn't swing the payments. We sold, broke even, and moved into the apartment. I didn't mind it for me, but I worried about Steven. There were some rough looking characters around sometimes. We never had any trouble, though. It took a while to figure out, but I think it was assumed that everyone there was in about the same boat. People left each other alone, which is as good as you can hope for, I guess. Except for when the last thing you want is to be alone.

One Wednesday morning, I recognized Erin's light knock at the door. I was wearing sweatpants and a Bears T-shirt and pouring Lucky Charms into a bowl, surely looking like an idiot.

"Hey," she said in the doorway. Her eyes looked naked, lids pink. Her hair was down and greasy. She was wearing her leather jacket. "I was wondering if you could give me a hand," she said.

They weren't the same boxes I had carried up the stairs those months ago, but they might as well have been. She pointed out the things to lift. Her car was small, a little Datsun hatchback, and we fit what we could and she said she'd figure out the rest later.

"It's my parents. They're freaking out." She pushed against the passenger door, jostling the boxes and bags we'd just stacked on the seat. "It isn't about you, don't worry. Nobody knows anything." She took out a cigarette and offered me one. I didn't have a light and so she lit both of ours. She cinched up her leather jacket against the wind. "They just don't think this whole thing is a good idea is all. They really want me to go to college."

It occurred to me that she was far closer to Steven's age than to mine. He'd be looking into colleges in, what, five years? Didn't seem possible. But if Erin took her time, went slow and worked, the two of them could see some overlap. She was so young. And yet, still, I didn't want her to go. I wondered if, in a way, I loved her. I leaned in and kissed her, not caring who might see. She reciprocated, but not much. She leaned back against her car and put her hands on my arms, patting them, keeping them down at my sides.

After a few seconds of silence I said, "Steven's going to miss you."

She took a drag of her cigarette and rolled her eyes and punched me lightly in the stomach. "Dads," she said, shaking her head.

—

I sat to the side of the front step while Kyle and Burt came in and out, loading things into some beater pick-up they'd borrowed. I moved further out of the way when they brought the furniture. My dad was up on the balcony, three floors above me.

"You sure you don't need help?" he called.

"No," Kyle said. "We got it."

When they brought the armoire down, Kyle set it on the truck bed and knocked on it with his knuckle. "Solid as oak," he said to my dad.

"Not really," my dad said and Kyle laughed. Then he called to my dad that he was going to drop the armoire and some other stuff off at Erin's parents' house. "Good man," my dad said to him.

I heard the sliding glass door shut.

Burt was in the passenger seat and the engine was running. It was cold and I'd been out there for a long time. Kyle tossed a few last things into the truck. Burt gave me a quick wave from behind the windshield, and a little smile. Kyle came up the front walk to where I was still sitting. "Got to go," he said, putting out his hand. I stood and shook it. He smiled and said, "Look, I'm still around. I'll get you a number as soon as I have one. We'll go up to the place."

"Okay," I said. I knew that this wasn't going to happen. He wasn't even sure where he was going to be living. "Are you sad about not being with Erin anymore?" I asked him.

"Yeah, man," he said. "Of course. It's the worst thing that's ever happened to me."

I thought about this for a second and then said, "My mom dying was the worst thing to ever happen to me."

Kyle put his two icy hands on my face, leaned down, and kissed me on my cheek, up near my left eye. His skin was soft and cold. To keep from crying, I said, "Gay."

I went back inside where it was warm. My hands tingled. At the top of the stairs, my dad was in the hallway.

He looked gigantic for some reason. The door to Kyle and Erin's apartment was open. The place was trashed. Bottles and cans were scattered across the floor. A torn Iggy Pop poster hung off the wall and ashtrays overflowed onto the carpet. There was a broken lamp in the corner. We both knew that the maintenance crew would pick up before the next tenants came in, but still my dad brought over garbage bags and our vacuum and other supplies and we did it in a few hours. When we left it was a lot better. There were stains on the floor and a big gray smear on the wall where Erin's writing used to be, and there was still the hole by the door, but just like the one in our bathroom, that was there when they moved in.

Domestique

The fields of corn turned to acres of trees as we entered the Shawnee National Forest, the shadows cooling us, the air now moist and carrying with it the clean smell of dark plantlife. The road felt good and I'd found my stroke. Even, on the down and the up. I was in that sweet spot, those hours after the first couple when your legs just keep going. Dory and I were side by side, matching up the wheels of our bikes and staying close. We played at taking off, only to slow, coasting back to the other and then picking up an identical stroke. *Whoosh* and *whoosh* and *whoosh*.

We were riding the height of Illinois, tip to top, Cairo to Chicago. Myself, Dory, and our friend Terry, who rode a Schwinn Le Tour III that had to be twenty, twenty-five years old. I have no idea when he'd picked it up. Sometime between his inviting himself along and the time we all hit the road, I guess.

Terry squeezed between us and called to Dory, "D'you see that woodchuck?"

"What?" Dory said.

"Woodchuck!" he shouted.

"I imagine there are a few of those around."

"D'you ever read *Walden*?"

She looked at him and then back at the road. "I think so."

"That part where he sees a woodchuck? And he wants to grab it and eat it right there, all raw."

"Yeah?" Dory called.

"It's the nature and the wildness he wants!" Terry yelled. "He just wants to eat it all!"

A trio of cars came up on us quickly and I dropped back so that my wife could get over. She did, but not before the guy in the third car laid on his horn good and long and I could see my wife's shoulders hunch in alarm. Her front wheel wavered just ever so little.

"Motherfucker!" Terry yelled at the car. He got up out of the saddle and pounded a couple strokes ahead of us, making a show for the guy's rear-view. He held up a fist and shook it cartoon-style. *Why, you…* I caught up to Dory once again and she tried to smile at me.

We stopped at the next picnicking area and ate some of what we brought: energy bars, smashed cheese sandwiches, apples.

"What was the name of that little dude?" Terry said, lighting an American Spirit.

"What little dude?" I said.

"That little dude from home. Little dude who disappeared."

I knew the person Terry was referring to. A boy from our hometown who went missing the year before. He was on his way home from school, middle of the afternoon. "Matt," I said. They found his body a few weeks later. "Matt something."

"Matt something, yeah," Terry said.

I waited a few beats for him to continue, but knew it was just Terry's brain and Terry's mouth doing what they do. He took a serious drag on his cigarette and blew the smoke in my direction.

I waved a hand in front of my face and said, "Come on."

"What? Don't be that guy." One of those ex-smokers, he meant. A hypocrite, he meant. Terry knows how to get to me.

Dory and I had been clean for three years by the time the summer of our trip rolled around. We'd been off everything: the booze, the pot, the coke, the X, the acid and mushrooms, the party-time whippets. Even cigarettes. One day we were Dory and Miro, that couple apt to take just about anything handed to them, and the next day—nothing. We gave up caffeine. We made a plan to quit and stuck to it even though our last night of indulgence we were both tired and only smoked a few bowls and cranked open a couple bottles of wine. It was a Saturday night and we passed out curled into each other on the couch. In comparison to how we felt most Sunday mornings, this next one was bright and sunshiny, this one was bluebirds on our shoulders, this one we walked outside onto our back porch and breathed in the city and it didn't feel polluted or hateful.

"You must have lungs of steel," Dory said to Terry.

"I'm still thinking about those woodchucks," Terry said. "That's the only part of the book I remember."

"Is that how you fancy yourself?" Dory asked. "Guy eating the woodchuck whole?"

"Oh, man," Terry said. He lay back on the dirt, one hand under his head. He smoked his cigarette and made no signal that he had anything else to say on the subject.

Dory walked across a field of thick grass. All around the perimeter of the field were gathering areas, metal roofs over concrete foundations and picnic tables. There were no people anywhere. Was it not summer? There should at the very least have been some teenagers hanging around taking care of their teenage business: smoking cigarettes and pot, shotgunning cans of Natty Light. Where have all the burnouts gone?

I asked Dory, "How are your legs?"

"Good," she said. "'They feel strong."

"We're making good time."

"I'm not worried about time," she said. A small group of birds fluttered out of one tree and perched in another.

"I think he'll calm down soon," I said. "Maybe tomorrow. He's just excited. You know how he gets. I guess that's the reason I couldn't tell him no."

"Miro, it's done," she said.

"He was so goddamn psyched about it."

I ran a hand over Dory's back. I took her hand and we lay on our backs watching the sky. I had to keep in mind these small moments with my wife. I knew she was telling the truth: it wasn't that she didn't want Terry there with us. The problem was that I allowed the meaning of the trip to be altered. The whole point was to do this alone, Dory and Miro, just us. To be alone while we still could. The plan, you see, was that when we got back to Chicago, we were going to start trying for a kid.

After five minutes, we got up and walked back to the shelter where we found Terry asleep on the ground, his limbs flung out into starpoints. His cigarette had burned down to the filter by where his hand lay palm up. His mouth hung open with his lower lip drooping, like someone still-framed a video of him getting decked with a doozy of a right.

A few hours later, we decided to camp just inside the Shawnee National Forest, only a half mile from where the woods end and the area gets back to the business of agriculture. From inside our tent, Dory and I heard the repeated chicking of a lighter and then smelled the pot smoke wafting from Terry's own nylon housing. Dory turned over in her bag. I whispered, "You know we can't ask people to change for us." We had to accept the fact that the world is full of temptation and that it is up to us to resist. Then I said, "It's just some pot anyway." In the morning, as we ate our breakfasts, Terry smoked up again, this time right in front of us. I said, "Can we keep that to a minimum?"

"Dude, I am," Terry said, and sucked on his bowl. He made a half-hearted effort to blow the smoke away from us, but the little wind there was brought it back. "I know you two are sensitive or whatever," he said. He put his stash back into his pack.

"You should come ride with us in the city," Dory said.

"I don't know," Terry said, yawning. "My asshole is killing me."

As we left the forest, we saw a small plane dusting the corn crops. It was sleek and modern looking, not the old biplane we all remember from *North by Northwest*. But old-fashioned or not, it was completely charming to a city kid like me. I pointed and smiled and waved at the unseen pilot. Terry seemed to take no notice of it. Dory tried to share in my enthusiasm, but she had fallen into a mood. The plane flew off and we continued down the road, inching towards the city.

Terry is my only friend—*our* only friend—from before we cleaned up. He and I went back to junior high. We played basketball together on the division's worst team three years in a row. We slept over at each other's houses and knew each other's parents as well, it seemed sometimes, as our own. We made out with girls for the first time on the same night, at a party in Terry's basement, sixth grade. Terry was with me, in fact, the night I met Dory.

We were twenty-three and looped on ephedrine and Mad Dog 20/20, coming in late to the California Clipper, watching some psychobilly outfit give bad medicine to the ghost of Hank Sr. Terry started dancing spastically (the only way he knew and the only style suitable for that music, really) and Dory, a stranger to us, joined him, matching his flailing arms and jerking legs. Of course I was attracted to her. I was twenty-three and fucked-up and Dory's a hell of a good looking woman. I've always thought so, though there have been periods when she looked less beautiful—a bit too much weight, or not enough, a little sallow in her face. I have no doubt she could say the same of me. There are pictures that make me cringe. But that night we were young and as beautiful as we ever were or ever would be. I figured if she was going home with anybody that night (she didn't) it would be Terry. He's handsomer than anybody realizes. If he could keep his mouth from falling slack or his eyes from going bloodshot, you'd see. The band finished up at quarter of two and Dory asked us to join her and her friends, who were not impressed by us or, it seemed, the larger world. The feeling was mutual. This was, in fact, the only time I would meet Dory's group of eye-rolling, cranberry-and-vodka high school chums. They didn't thank me when I bought a round of drinks I couldn't afford. They looked away while speaking to me in clipped, one-word responses. Dory, though, she looked me straight in my double vision. After a while, she and I were bringing each other drinks from the bar and it became clear that we'd hit upon something, she and I.

This is the only story I'll tell from those days, the only one I ever tell. Unfortunately, people want to hear the other ones: humorous tales of good nights gone bad, of near-misses, of bizarre cross-town cab rides and kooky dealers. We know, though, all too well, what's on the flip side of these anecdotes: the men and women playing chicken with a world of broken minds and tainted dope and unemployment and untold loss. We cannot tell these stories anymore.

When it comes down to it, we quit because it we had to. Individually, sure, we could have kept on with the lifestyle a few more years, another decade—hell, maybe more. Maybe until we were gray and the damn stuff started to blow out our organs and then, eventually, put us down in the ground. But *us*? We were quickly hurtling toward the end. As wonderful as it was over the first few months, as much as we felt we'd found an extraordinary adoration in the space between us, we also found a capacity for meanness, the sort of cruelty you reserve for the ones you love the most. It was getting to where every night we would find some reason to turn on each other. Screaming matches neither could fully remember in the morning. Cheating. Who cheated first I couldn't tell you. There's no thought happening in the moment, no concept of ramifications. Once I hit her. She had fucked so-and-so or I thought she wanted to fuck so-and-so. A slap, really. And in my very weak defense, she had taken to hitting me quite often (the first time was shocking, but after that it just became a part of the sad routine). But that, as memory serves, was the loudest alarm. She stood there with a hand on her cheek and we both knew that it was either the booze and the drugs, or us.

—

It was turning into a beautiful day, the sun high and bright, the air cool. Perfect. I came alongside my wife on the road and handed her a gel pack. She hadn't eaten much that morning and I knew she would run out of steam soon. Most people don't understand how a cycling team works. They think each rider is out there on his or her own, but there is careful coordination at work. Riders offer themselves as windbreaks for their teammates, taking turns drafting. And there's a member of every team who only supports the other riders. He's referred to as the *domestique*. This is the guy who fetches water and bars and gels from the team car and darts up through the crowded peloton to deliver them to the riders who have a chance to take the jersey. It's a necessary, if less than glorious, position. This is the role I find I naturally move to in awkward group circumstances, so over the next two days as we meandered in a general northward direction, switching from rough country roads to the shoulders of small highways, I gave myself to the team. I waved down cars to ask for directions when we became confused by the vast, unmarked intersections. I paid for more than my share when we stopped in small towns to eat and camp in KOAs. I filled up our water bottles at gas stations, leaving my teammates to relax outside. On the road, I offered food from my pack.

People in restaurants and shops were impressed by our trip, looking at our bikes and our gear and nodding their heads in some sort of appreciation. Terry was drinking and smoking each night, passing out and snoring clear through until morning, when he would wake and hack and spit into the grass outside his tent. Dory and I avoided each other's eyes.

—

So much of that trip was spent watching the gray road blur by just beyond my front wheel, and life rarely tells you that something special is about to happen. "Get ready," it does not say. "You're going to want to remember this." So all I can report is a mixture of memory flashes and information I've received since. I do know that on that fourth morning Dory had taken the lead and I was behind her with Terry bringing up the rear. We were on a bigger road than we'd have liked, but you can't always demand the most perfect conditions. It was a four-lane with a decent shoulder and a wide, grassy median between the directions. There was a little traffic, mostly long-haul trucks that had the good graces to merge left as best they could when passing us. For about a half hour I'd been having trouble switching between gears. Not that I needed to change all that often; the landscape of central Illinois is famously pancake flat, just excellent for cycling in my opinion, but I can be a stubborn son of a bitch and something of a fiddler and instead of leaving it alone, I was clicking back and forth, looking down at the chain as it unstuck itself and changed up and down the gears. I was about to ask Dory and Terry if they'd mind stopping so I could have a look at my derailleur when Dory said, "Hey." She said it quite calmly, though loud enough for us to hear above the wind of our movement.

By then the presence of those small, yellow crop dusters had become old hat and none of us were very impressed with that sign of country life that had so delighted me only a couple days before. But I looked up just in time to see, not fifty yards from us, a duster coming in low over the road, getting lower. It angled itself and then like a bug into a zapper smashed into the trailer of a semi-truck coming in our direction on the other side of the highway. A miracle of chance. The collision made an awful noise, explosive and ear-twisting. Dory screamed and we both crashed to the road. Much of the body of the plane went straight through the trailer, landing in a fiery crash on the other side. The impact pushed the truck onto its side and into the deep ditch lining the road. The wings of the plane sheared off and jagged hunks of fiberglass were sent hurtling across the area, slamming into the ground all around us. One of those pieces hit Terry squarely in the legs, flipping him and his bike over, landing him on his shoulder and smacking his head against the hot, black pavement.

For a moment there was deep silence, like the darkness past a flame. Then the sound came back, cars screeching, voices yelling. The sounds of disaster.

I couldn't say how long the ambulances and police cars and fire trucks took. Maybe a while, given that we seemed to be a few clicks outside of nowhere. I crawled to Dory, whose legs were good and tangled in her bike. I might have asked her if she was okay, or I might have just known by her expression. I looked back at Terry. He and the bike were twisted at gruesome angles. We got to him slowly—I'd find out at the hospital that my wrist was sprained and both Dory and I were patched with scrapes and cuts and bruises. But Terry was unconscious. There was blood on the ground, not much, just a thin spot, but it was enough to hold my focus for a long half-second. Dory said, "Don't move him." Cars stopped and strangers' faces moved in close to ours. Soon the road was as crowded as a backyard gathering, with folks in pairs and trios, many of them talking on phones or taking pictures with them The police were there a few minutes before coming to us. We must have blended in with the onlookers—just three cyclists down the road a bit watching the action. A man standing near to us waved his arms and yelled towards the cops. Soon Dory and I were being helped into the back of an ambulance while paramedics were carefully separating Terry from his machine. Dory and I were treated quickly. The police took our statements in the emergency room waiting area.

"Is there a family member you know of that we should contact?" the police officer asked. Terry's family was small: no brothers or sisters, no aunts or uncles that I ever met or heard of. His parents were always old—they must have been nearing forty when they had him, compared with mine who had me when they were barely into their twenties. His father passed away a few years before. His mother had a stroke shortly after and was in assisted living. I didn't know where this was, but told the cop that I'd try to find out.

Then, finally, they let us speak to a doctor. He was a frail looking old man, about sixty, sixty-five. Too old for an emergency room, that's for damn sure. I worried about what kind of treatment our friend was getting in this tiny hospital in this nothing burg. "Should he be, I don't know, airlifted somewhere?" I asked. "Cook County?" The doctor looked at me over his reading glasses.

"Your friend has a broken ankle, a fractured femur, fractured collar bone, and a fairly serious concussion," he said. "That sounds like a lot, and it is. But each injury is independent and each one we are more than capable of treating here. You can arrange for whatever you like, but I have serious doubts about anyone's insurance covering an unnecessary air transport." He paused to let his point make its way into my understanding of the situation. I was then stuck wondering what the chances were that Terry had any insurance at all. "He'll have to stay here for at least a few days. His legs have been reset. There's little we can do about the collar bone. Just have to wait for it to re-fuse on its own. He is under sedation right now, and on a good deal of pain medication." He said we'd be able to see him the next day, but that for now what he needed was rest.

A nurse appeared and said, "You folks can take his things and bring them back when he's ready to be discharged." She pushed his raggedy pack, even more raggedy now—broken straps, a rip in the outside pocket—out from behind the counter of her station and directed us to a motel about a mile up the road. Outside, Dory and I found our bikes leaning near the emergency room entrance. I sat Terry's bag on my crossbar and tied the straps to the handlebars. Dory and I slowly walked the bikes in the direction of the motel. It was dusk then, the sun setting on the west side of the flat, corn-and-soy horizon. I loved this landscape, still do. Even at that moment, with the pain of my own minor injuries finally finding the surface of my consciousness, I found it devastatingly beautiful.

It was dark by the time we got to the motel, a decent-looking place just off a highway overpass, surrounded by gas stations and fast food joints and liquor stores. We checked in and were happy to find a Mexican restaurant attached to the lobby. The clerk at the front desk said, "You two look like you've had a day. Where you headed?"

"Chicago," I said.

"Not the whole way on *bikes*." And there was that look— the dropped jaw, the tilted head, that expression of approval, even some sort of pride. But then that changed and she said,

"You all the ones out there on the road?"

"Yeah," Dory said.

The woman held a hand to her mouth. "How is your friend?"

Whatever this town was, it was small. "He's okay," I said. "They're keeping an eye on him."

We took the elevator up and dropped our bags onto the floor of our room. My wrist throbbed. I lay down on the bed. It was the softest thing I'd ever felt. Dory turned the light on by the sink and, wincing in front of the mirror, carefully removed her jersey and shorts. Dory's limbs are long and thin. A real cyclist's body. She pulled her hair back into a ponytail, revealing her neck to me. Because of her position by the mirror, I could see almost all of her at once. Both of us had crashed our bikes before. Anyone who rides as much as we do has stories of car doors flung open, of indecisive squirrels, of cell phone drivers turning without checking their mirrors. We've crashed together even, a few times, both of us limping home, taking turns sitting on the side of the tub while the other stung our scrapes with Bactine and covered them with gauze. We're used to seeing each other banged up. But this was different. Terry was perhaps ten yards behind me, maybe fifteen from my wife. Dory's bruised back and scratched arms and legs only made me think of how it could have so easily been her or me.

Still undressed, Dory turned to me, leaned against the sink counter. "We're going to have a baby, right?" she said.

"That's the plan, isn't it?" I said.

"Yeah," she said "Have you really thought about it, though? Do you know that that's what you want?"

"Of course I have," I said. "Yes, of course it's what I want." I don't know if this was true or not. Looking back now I think that this was an unfair question. Until the actual experience comes you can think of it in only the vaguest hypotheticals.

You cannot know what it is to have a child, *your* child. You cannot really understand the hours and the worry. And the joy. Had I thought about it? Yes. Did I know what it would be like enough to make a fully informed decision, to weigh the pros and cons, to be *sure*? Not even fucking close. Neither had she and neither has any first-time parent in the history of the world. This is my firm belief. We have babies on instinct. We have babies because we have babies because we have babies. So we can all keep going.

Dory moved away from the bathroom, towards me, and for a second I thought that she wanted to start the baby-making right then, and though normally I would have been all for it (there's something about the familiar anonymity of hotel rooms that has always urged us to be a little more adventurous in bed), my body was feeling sore and increasingly stiff. But she did not come to me. Instead, she walked to where the packs and panniers were piled on the floor. She crouched down, unzipped the front pocket of Terry's pack, and pulled out his knitted Guatemalan stash bag.

"I'm going to smoke Terry's pot," she said. She came and sat by me on the bed and went about packing a bowl.

"Babe," I began, but didn't continue. I was too tired to think. I couldn't think anymore about babies or Terry or meetings or the utter nonsense of seeing a plane fly into a truck. Three years since we'd indulged in anything, but Dory did not hesitate before lifting the pipe and Terry's Bic lighter to her face and taking a good-sized hit. She was resolute. She held the smoke in her healthy lungs for five seconds and then coughed it out. She took another drag and then put the pipe down on the bedside table and stood the lighter up next to it. The earthy cloud of smoke hung in the air like an old song.

I picked up the bowl and took a deep hit and then another. "It's good," I said. Dory lay next to me and then reached across my body for the bowl. She got a small drag and said, "Cashed."

I reloaded it and we did a couple more rounds. We fell further into the bed. I put my good arm around Dory's shoulder, careful not to touch any of her sores. After a few minutes, she said, "It just became very apparent that we haven't eaten anything today."

I splashed cold water on my face and we each got dressed. All we had with us were running pants and T-shirts. Her's was from a 5K run she did for breast cancer. Mine said Circuit City. I got it when we signed up for a credit card. Dory looked at me and then herself in the mirror. "Jesus," she said.

The host at the Mexican restaurant sat us in a booth and we ordered plates of enchiladas, chips and salsa and guacamole, and large glasses of water. "And a margarita," Dory said to the waitress.

"Little or big?"

"Big."

"Extra shot of Cuervo for two dollars."

"Yeah," Dory said, a sort of amused resignation in her voice. "Alright."

I held up two fingers at the waitress. When they came, the drinks were comically enormous. They were fish bowls. They were aquariums. God, what a world.

We could have said that we were doing this because of the stress of the day, because we were worried about Terry. We could have said that it was all just a pile of bad luck: the plane and us being there in a hotel room with a sack of weed. What were we supposed to do? We could have said that it was because we'd never had a proper send-off for our wild past, that we'd fallen asleep too early that last night (something that I had, in fact, come back to in memory, a regret for not having gone out in some great firework of consumption). We could have told ourselves and each other that we were high and getting drunk because we were going to have a baby someday soon and we were frightened as hell of that. And we would have been right about all of those, each one. But to be honest, we would have also had to admit that we were doing this because we both love the feeling of it. We love the fluid change from one state to another. We love the way the drugs and the booze cradle us in their chemical arms. We would've had to, for what surely would have been the thousandth time or more, admit our helplessness. But we did not want to admit that, not this night. So we shut up and drank.

After dinner, without discussion, we moved from our table to the dark wood bar with piñatas hanging above it. Dory spotted a juke box and while she punched in some tunes I ordered beers and two shots of tequila from the bartender, a woman in her forties, early fifties. There were three other drinkers there: to the right of us was an old man in jeans and flannel and a mesh-backed cap that said Jefferson Elementary; and to the left was a couple, a little older than Dory and me. They were clean-cut in chinos and blue polo and white shorts and red blouse. A good, healthy flag of America. The two men were both drinking beers. The woman sipped at a tall, wet glass of white wine. "Midnight Rider" drowned out the mumbling TV newscaster in the corner. Dory got back and we ceremoniously did our shots and sucked on lime and each had a slug of beer. Dory sang along to the lyrics she knew from the song ("I've got one *mooore* silver dollar") and then laughed.

"Did you know," she said, "that two members of the Allman Brothers died in separate motorcycle accidents in almost exactly the same spot, almost exactly a year apart? Isn't that nuts? What are the chances? Both of them, riding along...the second Allman must have thought, 'Well, it's not gonna happen twice' and then wham!" She clapped her hands together. "Crash!"

"You talking about the plane?" the old man in the cap asked us. We looked over. "Duster that went down?"

"Oh, we heard about that," the woman on the other side

of us said, leaning into the bar to see the old man past Dory and me. Her husband turned toward us slowly, looking like he'd just been left in mid-sentence.

"Something," the old man said, as in *Isn't life some kind of something?*

"You two heard about this, right?" the husband said to us.

Dory squinted her eyes towards the bottles behind the bar. "I think so," she said.

"You'd know it if you did," he said. "Goddamn plane flew into a truck. Right up the road. Exploded all over the place. Knocked the truck ass over tit."

"God," his wife said in a plaintive tone. "You know what it reminds me of."

"I know, I know," her husband said, putting an arm around her.

"The *plane*," she said, "and it's like, whoa, flashback. As soon as I heard about it, I just could help thinking about that morning, what we were seeing on TV. We were watching the second plane live," she said towards us and the old man, then turned back to her husband. "I mean, not like we were the only ones, but still."

"This must have been much, much smaller, though," the husband said.

"Well, of course I know that." His wife gave him a playful smack on the arm. "But still. *Similar.*"

I have to admit that I'd had the same thought. Not at the moment of impact, but sometime in the hospital or in the ambulance on the way over. Specifically, I'd thought of that field in Pennsylvania and I was struck by the weight that it still puts on my heart. To imagine the experience.

We drank and more songs came on: Bob Seger and Fleetwood Mac. Cat Stevens.

"Do we know what happened to the driver?" Dory said to the others at the bar.

"Going to have a mess of hospital bills, that's for sure," the old man said. "They said he got his arm stuck under something, all twisted out of sorts. Took a shot to the head when the damn thing went over. Man's gonna have a hell of a time with the insurance companies, too, on top of it all. Cocksuckers."

The word entered the conversation like a flung knife. Dory looked back and forth between the old man and the couple. I kept my eyes on her. My tolerance was on the floor and I was fairly drunk. That gorgeous feeling. My beautiful friend.

"That man can use some praying for, I'd say," the woman said, mending the breach of etiquette in our small community.

"You have to wonder what happened," the husband said. "Mechanical error or what. What was going on in that plane?"

"McIntire says he didn't see anything wrong with Grady this morning." The old man held up his beer bottle and the bartender brought him a fresh one.

The husband ordered another and I made a circling gesture around our bottles and shot glasses. The bartender went to work.

"Sorry," the husband said, getting back to the conversation. "Who's this you're saying?"

"Grady," the old man said, a bit annoyed. "The pilot. McIntire said he seemed fine, not looking ready to keel over or anything."

"Did he seem...distraught?" the woman said.

"Didn't say anything about that."

"And this McIntire?" the husband asked.

The old man looked past Dory and I at the husband, square in the face. "Guy whose fields Grady was doing," he said, tired of all these nonsense questions. "Just over across 20." I liked this old man. He was a real asshole.

"We're from Dayton," the husband said, explaining

his ignorance. The old man turned his eyes to the television. "Hell," the husband then said after a moment. "Oh hell, you're the ones that were out there at the accident. Aren't you? Remember," he said to his wife, gesturing toward the front desk of the motel, "she said that there were three people out there. They're the people on bikes."

"Is that true?" the woman asked us. The old man turned away from the TV to look our way also.

Dory ordered another round of shots. The husband said, "You deserve that. Day you've had."

"You should have told us," the woman said, perhaps a bit more seriously than she wanted. She finished her glass of wine and then made a smile appear.

"What were you people doing riding bicycles out there?" the old man said.

"Just heading home," Dory said.

—

Drying out had been tough, I'm not going to kid you. We knew it would be. In the hours leading up to our breakup with all things altering, I had dreadful images of us in opposite corners of our shithole apartment, sweating and trembling, sucking down mouthwash or combing through the carpet for any stray sliver off a pill. It wasn't quite like that. In reality, except for our meetings and work, we basically just stayed home. We watched a lot of movies and syndicated reruns. It was incredibly boring. There were moments I was at the door, hand on the knob, ready to find one of our dear, fucked-up friends, anyone who was holding anything. Or just hit the bar and toss back one whiskey after another. I didn't. We were miserable and we snapped at each other. We blamed one another, claiming the other's weakness to be more desperate than our own. We brought up the times prior to our meeting, mentioned how *fine* everything had been, how well we could handle ourselves. All bullshit, of course. We'd never been okay, neither of us.

But somehow we rode it out. After a few weeks my hands were still and my eyes clear.

Dory bought us the bikes as wedding gifts. "We need something to focus on," she said. She was right. Since quitting drugs Dory finished her degree in counseling and was interning at a clinic. I had somehow fallen into computers and took an IT position with AT&T. We bought a two-bedroom condo in Bucktown.

Cycling became what we looked forward to. We rode up and down the lakefront. We participated in monthly Critical Mass gatherings, hundreds of riders taking over Friday rush hours on the streets of Chicago. From early spring to the near-dead of winter we rode every chance we got. And when we weren't riding we were looking through cycling magazines, reading the glut of biographies of LeMond, Obree, Lance. We got cable so we could watch the major races in Europe and California. We discussed the doping scandals, so many people feigning disbelief and *tsk-tsk*ing the latest poor, stupid sap to get caught.

—

The old man and the couple all left the bar soon after it became clear that we weren't going to reveal any details about the strange incident on the road. Also, Dory and I were getting to a point of inebriation that is uncomfortable for most people to look at. I continued to be nearly completely silent and Dory started singing the wrong lyrics to songs. When they were gone we ordered another round and the bartender told us that this would be the last, that she was closing up.

That might have been the night we conceived our son. For a while leading up to his birth I'd hoped it hadn't been— sloppy, blurry, drunk sex, a little aggressive, me taking forever to finish—but when he arrived all those worries drifted away, as he was perfect as far as I could see and he had a good set of lungs to holler at the world. It could have been any of the next few nights, though.

We woke up in a headachy fog. I stumbled naked to the bathroom and made myself throw up and felt a little better for it. I then remembered hearing Dory do the same in the middle of the night, though whether hers was self-induced I can't be sure. Aside from the physical symptoms, we were both feeling the blues that used to only follow a good, long drunk. We said little that morning, showered and got dressed. I brought glasses of water from the bathroom and we slowly drank as much as we could. Outside, we hung the panniers on our bikes, strapped on our packs, and headed down towards the hospital to see Terry. Trucks rushed by us, loud and close. It occurred to me that this was the first time I'd ever ridden with a hangover. Two sides of my life came together with queasy and heart-palpitating results.

The hospital, now in the daytime, was a squat, yellow brick trio of buildings, acres of corn surrounding it. We signed in at the nurses' station and spoke with the old doctor who told us that the concussion was not as bad as they'd feared.

"He'll need help for a while," the doctor said. "Eating, bathing."

"Yeah, yeah," I murmured, "of course."

The doctor looked untrustingly at my beat-up, bedraggled ass.

In his room, Terry was propped slightly in the bed, an IV drip in his arm. There was a bandage over his forehead and squares of gauze on his face and chest. Both legs were casted and suspended. His right shoulder was wrapped. The sight was terrifying. His face was stubbled with beard. Beneath that his skin was gaunt. He looked like he was coming off one of our old lost weekends. There in the hospital room I realized how valuable Terry had been to us. All these years, as I judged and clucked my tongue at my old cohorts who had kept at the game of indulgence, I saved Terry for myself. Dory and I both did. We'd kept him and ignored all of his behavior, excusing it as some joke, everything that made Terry Terry. We lived through him, forgetting our ten-thirty bedtimes and flirtations with veganism, forgetting the goddamn bikes. We could once again, for our moments with him, mix drinks and snort lines, slip cigarettes from hardpacks and joints from pouches and light them, taking in big, harsh lungfuls of smoke. This was what he did for us. And after he was gone, we could sit for a moment and say, "Boy, that Terry sure needs to clean himself up," before turning to the news or talking about what to name the baby.

Terry raised his left hand about three inches off the bed and made something like a circular motion. "I'm all fucked up," he slurred.

"You'll be alright," I said.

"It's just the drugs," Dory said.

"Yeah," Terry said. Without moving his head, he looked over toward the window. "Is it today still?"

"No," I said. "It's tomorrow. You have to stay a few more days."

"Ah, that's okay," he said, flopping his hand down to the mattress. "I'm all fucked up."

His food came and we helped him eat three spoons of apple sauce, and then watched him fall asleep.

At the nurses' station, we borrowed a phone book and called a rental car company and booked a wagon big enough for our bikes. I hung up and the nurse said to us, "Police are saying suicide." She looked up from her computer screen.

"The pilot. They made an announcement earlier this morning. Said he wrote a letter. His wife left him and he couldn't make his mortgage."

So, it wasn't chance. It wasn't an improbably freak occurrence. There was, instead, according to this nurse, a mind behind the act. There was no accident at all. It was meant and purposeful. It felt like this news was supposed to change how we understood of the incident, but, I thought, what could the difference possibly be to us? We, who happened into the situation, who had no idea who the players were, who didn't even know where we were—what did it matter to us whether it was a mechanical disaster or the will of a devastated man? Either way it left no control in our useless hands.

The nurse smacked the clipboard on the counter and I jumped. "Sign out," she said.

"We're coming back," I said. "We're coming back to get him."

"It's fine," Dory said, and wrote our names next to our names.

The rental car people came, and we loaded our bags and bikes and began driving northeast. Soon we were on I-55, cruising at 70, 75 miles per hour, the radio nattering on, neither of us speaking. It was another hot one, and getting hotter. We rolled up the windows and put on the AC and I had trouble seeing the world outside as real. It was as if I was passing through an imaginary landscape. I sat back into the cushy drivers' seat, my right foot barely pressing on the gas pedal.

We got to the city in no time, but I wasn't ready to be back. I didn't want to see our apartment, our furniture, the way I knew the light would be coming in the kitchen window. I was about to head north on 90, towards our place off Fullerton, but Dory said, "No, keep going. Go on up to Lake Shore."

Relieved, I did so without questioning. Dory directed

me, with slow movements of her hand or a whispered word, down Lake Shore Drive all the way to Hyde Park. We stopped at Promontory Point and looked out at the lake. There were few people out: a couple homeless-looking men; joggers going by; mothers in yoga pants pushing strollers.

"There's a meeting at eight," I said. "The place near Belmont."

"Yeah," Dory said, and nodded her head. Then she grabbed her bag from the back and there in the passenger seat she tugged off her pants and shirt and wriggled into her kit. "Alright," I said and did the same. Neither of us had checked our bikes since we hit the deck the day before, so we flipped them over and went to work. We checked our cranks and cables, spun the wheels and tested that the derailleurs were doing their job, that the brakes weren't rubbing. The chains were good. Out on the trail the fresh lake waters slapped and smacked against the rocks, tossing up a fine spray. The moisture on the air woke me up. It was a Thursday afternoon, but the notion of days and times of day felt somewhat silly just then, the way an earlier argument can seem ridiculous after making love.

We rode north past the museums and the aquarium, the old Meigs Field, then Navy Pier with its Ferris wheel turning joyfully, mindlessly. The skyline came more into focus, gaining detail with each push on our pedals. It's a beautiful path along the lakefront, smooth and wide. As we got further north and passed the big beaches, the trail became crowded with joggers, skaters, other cyclists, Dory and I slowed and let our legs move in languid circles. Everyone looked to be in love with the city and the summer. To our right, the water was green-brown, as it always is, and I thought of how many animals and plants lived below the surface, how teeming with little bitty creatures it was. I'd read an article that said we only understand about half of what's in the ocean. There are hundreds of thousands of fish and plants and microbes that we haven't imagined yet. But they're there, living and eating and reproducing. I thought about the small, motivated little things crawling through the sand. I thought about the dirt of the cornfields we'd ridden past, about all the systems of life happening invisibly, food chains and splitting cells. And inside of us—all the blood and veins and specialized organs. I thought about how little I understood of my own body: how many bones I have, what my spleen does, how smell works. What I had done to my body through all the years of chemical abuse. I thought about the night before and my sperm and genetic dispositions, about traits passed on from one generation of animal to another.

When we got to Montrose Harbor, Dory stopped. I pulled beside her and saw she was crying. "It was a plane and a truck," she said. "What the fuck are we supposed to do about that?" She pulled the collar of her jersey up and wiped her eyes. "We'll have to take care of him," she said. "He'll be helpless."

She was talking about Terry. And of course she wasn't.

We rode back to the car and then drove to our place. We slept and then woke and made love. We ordered in food from the corner and ate on the couch, watching the evening news. Later that night, we went into the all-purpose room at an Episcopal church and looked at our watches and announced how long it had been since our last drinks.

We picked up Terry from the hospital three days later and set him up on our sofa, where he stayed for four weeks, seeming to enjoy the attention and care we gave him. He fell into our routine, minus the cycling of course. Surprisingly, he never said a word about wanting a drink or even a cigarette. I thought I caught a faint whiff of vodka coming off him a few times and then I wondered who might be visiting in the hours Dory and I were at work, but mostly he lived soberly and uncomplaining. When Dory and I got married, Terry showed up late to the wedding, obviously drunk. Our new friends, ones we had met at meetings, tried to talk to him about control and powerlessness, but he only laughed and clapped them on the back and walked away. Now with him on our couch, I came back to this and wondered if there was something he knew that I never would. He was the first person we told about the baby, when it was just nestled in Dory's womb.

One night Dory had gone to bed and Terry and I were watching TV and he said, "I wish I had gotten to keep that piece of wing."

"Yeah?" I said. "Souvenir?"

"Oh, man," he said.

A headlight swung in from the street and someone on the TV said something and right then I knew that after he left on his own two legs, we would probably never see Terry again. There in our living room I felt a sort of mourning weight on my chest over how much I would miss him, how much Dory and I both would, and how hard it was going to be adjusting to a life without him.

The Tall Lake Grasses

Until nearly one, Beth watched as the police came and went from the McKenzies' house across the street, in and out the front door, through the garage, around the back and into the woods behind their house, yellow spots of flashlight cutting up and down the trees. She finally fell asleep on the floor, the rotation of red and blue lights no longer alarming, but instead luring her away from consciousness. In the morning there was no news. The boy, Matt McKenzie, was still missing, having not come home from school the day before. He was last seen—by Beth, as it happened—walking along the bike path that ran twenty-five miles, through four towns, and which passed only yards from the McKenzies' home. At six-thirty, first light, the people of the town woke and, realizing that his disappearance was not some prank, some mix-up, dressed and prepared for the day.

Beth went downstairs, still in her pajamas, and her mother was in the TV room looking out the window. The action of the search seemed to be nearing full swing. Across the street, people approached the house and were sent away by the police, pointed east toward the school and the town. Her eyes still gunked with sleep, Beth could not recognize who they were, the ones coming to help.

"No school," her mother said. It was a Friday. "People are gathering there, though. They said that was the best place to start, spreading out along the bike path."

The smell of coffee was so strong on the first floor it swaddled Beth's head like a wrap. She went to the kitchen and poured half a cup, filled the rest with milk and two spoons of sugar. "Honey, I wish you wouldn't," her mother said, looking down at the cup as Beth returned to her side at the window. But they both drank and watched. "That trail," her mother said. "We should go help out."

"Guess so,"

"Stick together."

Beth scrunched her face and rolled her eyes. "Obviously."

"I'm serious. Threes. Or fours."

Beth texted with her friends. Caitlin wrote *b ther in 20.* Steph wrote *ware suit.* She showered and dressed, her two-piece under tank and cut-offs. She waited on the porch, the commotion across the street coming in waves. She prayed she wouldn't be the one to find the kid.

Her mind rewound to the previous afternoon and what she had seen as she rode away from school down the bike path that led to their neighborhood. Matt was walking not far from the mouth of the path. She came up from behind him and did not recognize him at first. But as she passed and his face became visible, she registered the boy. Beth babysat Matt for a short period a couple of years before. Though she was only a few years his senior, the McKenzies paid Beth seven dollars an hour to spend evenings with him while they were out. Matt was small and a bit rodent-like, with a pointy face and limp, thin hair the color of wet cardboard. Just a freshman now, he seemed to have spent this first year in a state of near-constant social panic. They did not speak to each other in school. Neither had ever even attempted.

Beth let her mind pass Matt by on the bike path. She tried to see the woods, her front tire spinning over the asphalt. Did she see anyone else? This was what the police had asked her the evening before. Did she see anyone else on that path? Any friends? Anyone from school? Anyone she did not recognize? Anyone at all? She replayed it: school, Matt, the woods. But she'd ridden that path so many times—hundreds, thousands— that her mind hardly took note. She swerved around the path's divots and raised scar-like cracks instinctually, certainly mindlessly. In this replay of the afternoon before, she simply arrived home. The ride had been perfectly eventless.

Steph and Caitlin got there along with Caitlin's mother and the group of women set off toward the high school. Though only May, it was hot. Summer came early and breathing fire. People criss-crossed the parking lot, some determinedly, some simply wandering in the morning light. A woman at an unfolded table told the women to take the north side of the path. "And stay together," she said. "That is incredibly important."

They walked distractedly for two hours, every once in a while being directed by one male adult or another to head down that way or double back over that embankment. They did as they were told, Beth figuring that one plot of dirt to shuffle across is as good as any other. Anyway, it was cooler in the woods. Standing atop the next hill, Beth saw her father standing with a group of men. She didn't recognize the others. They were taking turns looking sadly at the ground and squinting deep into the woods. Beth's father was not a person she thought of very often. He was a nice man, caring father, she supposed, a hard worker as far as she ever knew, but when she thought of her family it was her mother who came to mind. It was always a mild surprise when she saw her father, as if they'd taken on a perfectly amiable, but unexpected overnight guest. A strange sensation, one that she had gotten used to years ago, but which never fully went away. She imagined that after she left the house, her parents would probably divorce.

By early-afternoon, nobody had found anything and people were meandering away towards their homes, calling it a day. Beth's mom said, "Well," and Caitlin's mother said, "Seems like we're covering the same areas over and over, doesn't it?" They headed to the lake while their men continued to search and find nothing.

The water was lukewarm and thick with algae. There wasn't much of a beach, but enough of a swath of sandy dirt to let them all make believe. A few old people were there, gathered together and talking about Matt McKenzie in hushed tones. Little kids splashed around in the shallows, floaties puffed around their arms, parents watching. There were no boats that day and so Beth took a good long swim out towards the middle. When she turned to come back she saw a figure waving at her near shore. He was separated from the rest of the suntanners by a bank of tall reeds that cut into the lake like a jetty. Beth squinted and then swam, slowed and squinted and swam. The figured waved on. It wasn't until she could touch the gooey bottom of the lake that she recognized him, a boy named Silver. He had just moved to her school that year, or maybe the year before. He was junior, like Beth. They had science together.

In a loud whisper, Silver beckoned Beth to come. He waved his cupped hand, said "Come here."

She came forward and stood as tall as she could. The brutal sun baked her shoulders. "You wish," she said, a hand on her submerged hip.

"I want to show you something," he said.

Beth sloshed through the shallows, the lake grasses

slicing softly at her legs. Everyone else was a good twenty yards off, around the curve of the small shore. The wall of reeds stood between them and where Silver was. Beth went to him, disappearing from the view of any of her friends. "Closer," he said.

"I am," she said, stopping six feet from him.

The water only came to his calf, where Beth was still up to her thighs. Silver was tall and thin. And he was ugly, Beth thought, with eyes close together and a too-wide jaw and pock-marked skin. So ugly. Not that Beth thought she was so very beautiful, but she never minded the look of her own face, and she thought her body had a decent shape. Plus, the boys seemed to like her fine. She'd gone out with a couple and had dates to the last two homecomings. She hadn't liked any of them, really, but it beat going alone or making Caitlin and Steph drop their dates so they could go as a group.

"Look at this," Silver said. From behind him he revealed a thin rope about two feet long, green marsh grasses braided together. It dripped with water from the lake. He raised his hand shoulder high and then whipped the rope behind him hard. It snapped against the skin of his back and his eyes clamped shut and his mouth pulled into a grimace.

"What the fuck?" Beth said, taking two clumsy steps away from him. "Why'd you do that?"

"I don't know," he said, almost laughing in pain. "It hurts really bad." He splashed down to his knees and limboed back so that only his chest and face were about the surface of the water. "Oh, man, that stings." The long, stretched expanse of his torso was fish-belly white in the high sun. "My heart's beating like crazy." She thought she could almost see this through the thin curtain of his skin. His eyes remained closed. He breathed in and out, his sunken chest holding a small pool of water like a tea saucer.

"If you're trying to get known as the weird kid, it's

working." Beth tried to see over the reeds to where her friends and mother were, but her toes only went deeper into the doughy pond floor. "I have to go," she said.

"Hang on," Silver said. He stood and seemed even taller than before. His hair was slicked down, parted down the middle, and she could see that his head was strangely shaped, pointy. "I thought I'd give this to you." He held out the grass rope. "I was just making it for something to do. Look," he said, and loosely wrapped the rope around his wrist a few times before tying the ends together. He slipped it over his hand. "Here. It's not a thing or anything. Just, whatever."

Beth took the bracelet and said again, "I have to go." She slogged through the soft lake bottom to her friends, who were just coming out of the water and dancing across the ground to where they'd set up camp. Steph and Caitlin and the two mothers all in a row. Beth got to them, slipped the bracelet under her towel, and lay down on her stomach, as if it was her own back that had been marked. Not far behind, the search party stomped through the brush of the woods.

—

The knot holding the braids into a bracelet was tight and complicated. Strands of lake grass twisted together and frayed, hiding the points where the two sides came together. Beth sat on her bed with her desk lamp shining down. She tried to use only the very tips of her fingernails to pick and pick at the knot. Finally, the two ends fell apart and the loops once again became a line. For some reason it seemed to Beth that it should suddenly take on more weight, but it was still light, as if it might float away.

There was something in the sound it made when it hit Silver's back, the immediacy of the boy's reaction, the way Beth could see the sensation consume his whole world. It distorted his face and, if only for a second, flung him away like a rock off a sling. It reminded her of times when she had to get shots from the doctor. The other children would cry and reach out to their mothers for help and protection, but the pain never bothered Beth. In some inscrutable way, she enjoyed it. In the years since, she had found moments of injury—a broken toe in gym class, a burn on her arm from a frying pan—somehow satisfying, comforting. These sensations concentrated the world into that pinprick, that fracture, that burn. It was like a television in an otherwise dark room, the way that bright light can black out everything around it.

She stood and turned and thwacked the rope against the bed. It made more of a thud than a snap, as it had on Silver's skin. She threw aside the bedspread and did it against the tight fitted sheet. This time it was sharper, and louder. Beth locked the door and turned the radio on. A pop song buzzed tinny through the room. She whipped the bed once more, putting her arm into it this time. It was dusk outside, the late summer sun finally settling away, the street and the McKenzie house darkening. The lights were on, as they had been since the evening before. Beth saw figures move across the windows. She twisted the blinds shut and turned her head to look in the mirror behind her. She pulled the back of her tank top up to her shoulders. She unhooked her bra, letting the ends dangle below her armpits, and raised the whip into position.

—

Silver's house was small—just one story—and old. The paint was chipped and the windows lent a wavy distortion to the view from outside to in. In the middle of their middle-class town, there was this stretch of a three blocks that called attention to itself with its ramshackle ranch cottages, its littered gutters, its barking dogs behind chain-link fences.

When Beth rode up just a few minutes before, she'd felt suddenly vulnerable in her pink Oxford blouse and her khaki slacks. She climbed the three steps and knocked on the door. It was flimsy, unexpectedly hollow, and it seemed as though her little knuckles could have gone right through. Up until the second the door opened, the moment she saw the gray face of the man look down at her, she did not know what she was going to say or even why she was there. But then the man said, "Hello," in a soft, but deep, almost guttural voice (he was surely Silver's father—she'd heard that voice in science), and Beth said, "I'm a friend of Silver's?" Simple. True. Kind of.

He turned and said, "Silver, are you here?"

Silver came into the hallway and a peered over his father's angular shoulder. "Oh," he said.

"A friend of yours?" his father said. He was looking at Beth. His eyes seemed to be touring her face and head, examining it as if it were an odd animal.

"This is Beth, Dad," Silver said. "Yeah, we're practically best friends." One side of his mouth curled.

Silver led Beth down a slightly musty-smelling stairway. "I live in the basement," he said, turning his head halfway.

"Of course you do," Beth said.

At the bottom of the steps, Silver had to lean his head sideways to fit into the squat room. It was big, much bigger than her or any of her friends' bedrooms, and all that space made it look empty. There was a bed, a dresser, two chairs— one upholstered, but thread-bare, and one that had been snagged from a dining room set—and a card table in the corner, a makeshift homework desk, but it was all terribly insufficient. The carpet was beige and dingy. Window wells let little light into the room.

Silver sat on his unmade bed, leaned over the side and plugged in the Christmas lights that were taped into a zig-zag across two walls. Beth thought of Charlie Brown's shirt. She sat on the straight-back chair.

"Did you know that kid?" Silver asked.

Beth said, "Not really," feeling as if she was lying and telling the truth at the same time. "So what's with 'Silver'?" she said.

"It's a family name."

"'Silver.' That's so weird."

Silver shrugged.

"You aren't wearing your bracelet," he said.

Beth pulled the grass rope from her pocket. "I don't want it," she said, holding it out to him. "Why'd you give it to me?"

He shrugged again.

"Why'd you hit yourself like that?" she said.

"I already said, I don't know."

She looked away and tried to not think of the pure, clear snap of the rope against her skin. There was a basket of laundry with a pair of dust-colored underwear on top. There was what looked to be mouse droppings in the corner.

"I kind of liked how it felt," he said. "It hurt in a really good way."

"You're such a fucking freak."

Silver slid off the bed onto his knees and shuffled across the carpet to her. Beth thought of how disgusting that carpet was. "You should get me," Silver said. He turned and pulled his T-shirt over his head. His long, gray swath of skin was spotted with pimples. God, Beth thought, how is it possible that he's even uglier from behind. The faint line from the day before still ran down his back. He curved forward and his spine pressed out of his skin. "Just once," he said. "Don't hold back."

Beth moved to get up and leave, but only got as far as taking in a deep breath. She sat up so that she was now practically looking straight down at his stippled back. "You're so…" she started. She held tight to the end of the whip and before she could let her conscience protest, she flung it forward and slashed at his skin. Silver sucked in through his teeth. Down the length of his back an inch-wide welt line rose. She put her hand out and placed two fingers on his skin, straddling the wound. "One more," he said. Beth whipped him again. It smacked loudly. The marks made a tall, thin X. "Ow," Silver said. "That's enough." He leaned further forward so his head was on the floor and started laughing.

"Okay, shut up," she said. She was breathing heavily. "Do me now." She moved to the floor, lay down, and wriggled her shirt up to expose her lower back. The carpet was crunchy against her stomach. She closed her eyes and saw in the darkness of her head the image of her own skin, pale and blank. She tried to see through Silver's beady eyes, what she might look like to him, where those eyes would go. The grass rope came down with a light *swack*. She sighed and said, "No, for real."

A few seconds passed, but she remained in place, determined to be patient. Then she felt the whip cut across her skin. Her eyes and mouth burst open, but she saw nothing, nor did she make a sound. She could not hear a thing, no movement, no breathing. She might have disappeared, she thought. She or the world or both. Become gone. The pain pushed out from the source in hot waves, like the wake off a vessel. She pressed her forehead into the carpet and concentrated all her mental energy on the sensation. After a few moments the undulating sting subsided and she was left with a simple channel of heat.

She found Silver sitting back on his feet. "Get me a mirror," she said. He popped up and moved to the basement steps with such speed and ridiculous abandon that he cracked his head against the stair overhang. "Ah," he said, putting a palm to his hairline.

"God, hurry," Beth chided him. "Before it fades."

When he returned, Beth craned her neck and gazed at the red mark with a kind of affection. She squinted her eyes and saw that there were even specks of deeper red within the stripe, tiny flecks where the skin almost broke.

—

Monday came with no word on the McKenzie boy. Reporters stood just off school grounds: a few men and women Beth recognized from the local news; a couple better-looking heads she suspected to be from national channels. Beth's classmates gathered around them waiting for their chance to get known. How many of these kids knew the kid? Beth wondered. She thought that he must have had friends, but for the life of her, she couldn't say who one might have been. He never had a visitor any of those few evenings they spent together. They never even really spoke to each other, just watched television and ate mac-n-cheese.

Beth had never talked to Silver either, had hardly taken notice of him, and now on Monday morning she had to busy her eyes with the books and folders she carried as she passed him in the hall. She sneaked looks at his table in the cafeteria, where he sat with other school unknowns, some of whom she went to elementary school and junior high with, and yet who still remained anonymous. (She tried to think if Matt sat there. But maybe he had lunch the earlier period.) Even hunched awkwardly over his pizza bread Silver towered above the other kids. He spoke with them intermittently and unsmiling—what did they talk about? Teachers, assignments. Matt McKenzie. What else? Did he say, "I had an interesting experience with a girl this weekend"? She looked for signs: hung jaws, nervous laughing, comical dropping of forks. She saw nothing, but still she watched and worried.

"I think it'll be this week," Caitlin said softly. "Dana's parents are going out. We talked about it." It was a discussion coming up on its three-month anniversary: should Caitlin and Dana do it?

"You should hold out for someone way better," Steph said. "Plus I'm pretty sure losing your virginity to a guy named Dana makes you at least part lesbian."

"Like Eric was such a catch," Caitlin said, and Steph turned her head away.

As for Beth, it wasn't as if she didn't care, but she hadn't been able to form an opinion. The topic made her uncomfortable and vaguely frightened. She thought of the boys she'd gone out with and tried to imagine wanting to be with them in that way. She looked over as Silver scraped a mound of coleslaw from his plate into the trash and set his tray on the conveyor.

That afternoon Beth met with the guidance counselor. He said they needed to work out a way for Beth to get her GPA up before applying to colleges the next year. Beth had always been a distracted and anxious student. Tests made her an insomniac. Papers became a mish-mash of half-asserted notions and hedged bets. "You're right on the border," the counselor told her. "How are you doing this semester?" She scrunched up the side of her mouth. "Well, we need to find a way to get the schools to notice you," he said. He said she needed extracurriculars. Did she like debate? Student Senate hold any interest? Sports? "We need you to be involved in the community of the school," he said "That's what they want to see, that you're not just another student. Too many kids, their transcripts read like they just get done each day and disappear."

As soon as the words left him, the counselor's face went slack. There was a taut line connecting his eyes to Beth's. "What I mean," he said, and then finally turned his eyes downward, away, and pinched the bridge of his nose. "Jesus Christ," he breathed to himself.

—

Again, Silver's father answered the door. All limbs, this guy. A regular Ichabod Crane. Just like his son. He raised his arm and pointed a long finger to the basement door all the while drinking from a steaming mug of coffee. Beth got halfway down the stairs and said, "Hey, it's me. Your dad let me in." She waited for a reply. "If you're doing something gross, stop it."

Silver appeared at the bottom of the steps. "What would I be doing?"

His room was tidier this time. The laundry was in a basket with a lid. No sign of mouse turds. "I saw you looking at me in the cafeteria," he said. Beth's body stiffened. She looked everywhere but at him. "I'm not going to say anything to anybody."

Beth examined the room, walked the perimeter. "Where'd you move here from?" Beth asked.

"Itasca." Beth didn't know where that was, but thought the name sounded exotic, all those vowels. "My dad got transferred and he didn't want to drive so far," Silver continued.

"Sucks," Beth said.

Silver sat down on the stiff straight-back chair. "Do you want to do it again?"

Their science textbook was on the card table, open to the chapter on black holes that they were supposed to read that week. "Where's your mom?" Beth said, turning the pages of the book.

"Let's just do this," Silver said.

"Does she live here?"

"Please," Silver said. He looked at her with those silly eyes of his, pleading, and then back to the carpet. She had stumbled upon something painful for him.

"Come on, where is she?"

No answer. Silver was rubbing the palm of one hand against the back of the other. Beth asked the question again. "Did you just come here to be mean to me?" Silver said.

"I'm not mean. I'm curious."

Silver sighed and told her, simply, that his mother was gone.

"Dead?"

"I don't know. I guess not. She left, like, eight years ago. I got a card from her once. I have a picture of her."

He began to stand, but Beth said, "I don't want to see it," and Silver sat down again.

She felt a twinge of regret at having pressed the subject. She knew, of course, that there was something wrong there. It was in the faint mildew stench, the dust that enshrouded most every surface. It was in the way Silver had cleaned up his dank basement and in what little difference it made. But mostly, it was the quiet of the place that tipped Beth off, and the fact that Silver's father hadn't yet opened the door to the basement and called out some excuse—a quick question for his son, an offer of lemonade—to find out what was happening down there. But she did not want Silver's story, not the specifics, did not want to see him get excited about some lousy picture of his deadbeat mom. Now that she had pushed him to open up, she did not want to know what variety of sadness had consumed this house.

On the card table was a stack of papers held together with a black metal clip. Beth squeezed the arms of the clip, slipped it off the papers, and hid it in the palm of her hand. She walked to where Silver sat and said, "Shut your eyes."

He raised his head, but did as she told him. Beth leaned

over and, with a bit of effort in her fingers, spread the clip. She carefully placed it around Silver's earlobe, and then let the contraption clamp itself down.

Silver's eyes opened and he stood from the chair and stomped his feet lightly in place. He raised a hand to the side of his head, but did not remove the clip. "Yikes," he said looking down at Beth.

"Damn," Beth said.

"Okay, take it off," Silver said.

"No, wait a few more seconds," Beth said. She placed her palms against his chest. "Five more." Silver cinched up his face. "Four," she said. "Three." She let the last two seconds expire in silence and then removed the clip. Silver's earlobe was red. She put her fingers to the satiny skin and found it hot to the touch.

She went to where she'd set her purse down on the floor and extracted the grass whip. "Now," she said. "But you should tie my hands first."

Silver froze for a moment like a confused pet. "With what?"

"Anything. It doesn't matter." He scoped the room and picked up a long, white tube sock from the floor. "Gross. Not that," she said. She went to his dresser and opened a drawer. She tore through his clothes and pulled out a yellow Oxford. "Use the sleeve."

He twisted the shirt around her wrists and tied a knot. The fabric was stretchy enough that she could have easily pulled her hands right out, but tight enough to give the impression of constraint. Beth kneeled on the floor and placed her bound hands on the bed. She laid her cheek on top of them. Silver's shirt smelled musty, as if it had been in the drawer for a good long while, but she could still detect laundry detergent beneath that stink. She wondered what bizarre off-brand detergent his father bought.

"You have to raise my shirt," she said. He stepped to her from behind and she felt the tips of his fingers drag across her skin as he pulled up. He stopped with her lower back exposed. "All the way," she said. A second passed before he stretched the shirt out and over her breasts and shoulders. "Undo my bra," she said. "But don't try anything creepy." After a bit of fumbling, he negotiated the snap and she took in a deep breath. Silver stood to her side and she could see his erection pushing at his khakis. She scooted back so that her shorts pulled down a bit, exposing a little more hip, another inch of skin.

"Do it," she said.

The first strike was low on her back, the end of the whip snapping against her tender side. "Again," she said. This one was higher. It felt as if the thing would rip right down to her ribcage. Her eyes watered.

"Is that too much?" Silver asked.

"It's good," she said.

—

Matt McKenzie's body was found two towns over two weeks after going missing. A man was walking his dog in a field. The dog bolted. When he got to the spot where the dog was barking and whining, even before he brushed away any of the dry dirt and leaves, the stench was overwhelming. According to reporters (whom Beth watched on the television in her bedroom and out the window where they stood stationed outside the McKenzie house), the body was severely decomposed, due to the soaring heat that late spring, forcing the police to consult the boy's dental records in order to make a definite identification. They estimated that he was killed only hours after leaving school. Beth thought of how they'd wandered the woods that Friday morning and how he was probably already dead by then.

There was no movement in the house across the street. Beth went downstairs and found her parents watching the news report. She could see in her mother's face that she'd been crying.

"Sit down here," Beth's father said. Beth sat between them on the couch. She wondered what it would be like if it were just she and him, like Silver and his father. He ran a hand over her hair and then kissed her on the temple. He rubbed her back and she almost jumped in pain when his fingers crossed her latest whip mark. "You okay?" he said.

"Yeah," she said.

"Little spooked by all this?"

That evening, Beth and her mother made three pasta casseroles, one for dinner that night, one for the freezer, and one to bring across the street. Out in the heat, Beth held the casserole dish with a kitchen towel while her mother knocked. A man she'd never seen before answered the door. Some uncle, Beth suspected. There were always uncles. Behind him was a house that Beth knew well, but now it looked strange. Perhaps they painted, she thought. Her mother explained quickly that they lived across the street and that they'd made this casserole and if there was anything else they could do. The man nodded as Beth handed over the dish. He quietly thanked them and turned back to the formerly familiar rooms. When they crossed the street, Beth found that the whole neighborhood seemed odd, as if it the light was coming from the wrong angle, making unnatural shadows.

—

The next day, Saturday, Beth went back to the lake. Her parents were at an emergency PTA meeting at the school. The night before, a handful of other parents from the street had gathered in their living room to discuss what safety measures they might propose. They talked about getting the neighborhood watch program going for real. "Something more than a sign every few blocks," one man said. "A patrol," another said. Beth had stood at the top of the stairs. The adults remained there until after midnight. In the morning, Beth found a collection of empty wine bottles in the recycling bin.

The police had declared a six p.m. curfew for anyone under eighteen and all residents were encouraged to stick to groups regardless of the time of day, reminding the town in press conferences that Matt McKenzie was abducted in the light of the afternoon. But Beth had seen enough television and movies to know that any sick fuck that wanted to snatch and kill (and whatever else) a thirteen-year-old boy would probably have little interest in a seventeen-year-old girl. They have types, is what she'd learned. She went into the already-sweltering morning and quietly cut down the McKenzies' driveway to the bike path.

The lake seemed to be abandoned even of sound. She waded into the shallows and collected the tallest, thickest grasses she could find and then sat on the dirt of the shore and began braiding a new rope. She made three braids and then twined those together, and then repeated the process until she had a whip the width of her index finger. She bent it this way and that and thwacked it against the dirt until it loosened. She swung it like a propeller above her head and then rolled it and squeezed it into the pocket of her cut-offs.

Making her way through the silent woods, back on the bike path, Beth turned a curve and gasped as she was met by the long, gray face of Silver's father. He stood as if he'd been there for some time, legs shoulder-width apart, his arms down at his sides, as if he'd been calmly waiting just for her. His face betrayed no surprise at her appearance, no twist of identification. She froze in place. Her hands and feet went numb. Her lungs were empty of air. It was then, in this split second, with three feet between her and this man, that she for the first time recognized what Matt McKenzie must have experienced: the terror that took hold of every cell of his body, the sudden understanding that horror and death might be real after all. Her heart thumped wildly. She was stuck to that place on the bike path, weighed down by all the evil of the world.

Silver's father continued to look at her and, finally, said, "Oh." He nodded once and walked around Beth. She remained there, imagining him coming to her from behind, pinning her arms back and pulling her off to some dark place.

But he did not come back. No one did. Not Silver's father, not Matt McKenzie's killer, not anyone. Beth stepped forward once and then again, all the while seeing in front of her the face of a boy she hardly knew at all. She saw his face the way she did the afternoon he disappeared, as she rode past him on this path. She went forward until the path opened up at Silver's street. She went to his house and turned the knob of the flimsy front door, went down the basement stairs and found Silver just sitting up. His face, so like his terrifying father, looked up at her in sleepy confusion. She lay down next to him in his bed and it seemed to Beth that instead of just a thin sheet, there was a wider swath of fabric over them, an endless blanket under which laid everything in her life: her mother and father, her friends, Matt McKenzie, his murderer, high school and college, boys she had gone out with and boys she had yet to meet, everything she feared and all could imagine for herself. In the midst of this cacophony of memory and thought, in this bed in this basement, Beth and Silver kissed and undressed. Their pale skin glowed. Their terrified hands brushed at each other's bodies—all that muscle and fat and hair and bone. All that skin. At moments it felt to Beth like a struggle, but at others it was more of a dance, a strange choreography of taking and giving. The act itself, the deed, ended nearly as soon as it began, and with a shot of pain the likes of which Beth had never felt before. When they were finished, they remained there for a good long while, holding tight to one another, as if each was promising to never let the other go.

—

The police caught Matt McKenzie's killer a month later. He was a man in his late thirties who worked at a large nondescript office park in the next town over. The news showed him being led into a police car, his head covered with a blue windbreaker. That night, after eating the pasta casserole from the freezer with her parents, Beth texted Caitlin and Steph about Matt McKenzie and his killer, and about Caitlin and Dana, who still hadn't done it. Beth looked up twice and found her mother's eyes on her. "Are you going to stare at me all night?" Beth said.

"Probably," her mother said.

Reporters lined up outside the house across the street, but the McKenzies were already gone, having slipped away earlier that day. Beth watched from her bedroom window until after eleven, when the reporters packed up their gear and drove their vans away, and the neighborhood was once again dark. She texted Silver to say goodnight, and then once more, just before falling asleep, to voice a thought that was lingering in her head, that there were just too many freaks in this world.

All We Have

Bob Reznik sat on the couch watching his son get pummeled on TV. Halfway through the second quarter, the Lions were already ahead 21-3, and Mike Reznik had just fumbled for the second time. He was still on the ground when the referee shot his arm toward the Lions' end zone, confirming the turnover.

What is going on here, Bill? the play-by-play announcer asked of his partner.

I'll tell you, Pat, his partner said. *What's going on here is that nothing, and I mean nothing, is going right for Mike Reznik and company. You've got receivers dropping balls, you got confusion in the backfield, no one is picking up the blitz, and at the center of it all is a young quarterback who can't scramble and who—as we saw just there—isn't feeling comfortable in the pocket either.*

But as you said, he is young.

He is young, but the fact is that he's the leader of this team and he's the one who needs to step up if they're going to turn this around, and that's something I have yet to see him do.

"Goddamn right," Bob Reznik said, not looking away

from the screen even as it went to commercial. "A thousand times I told the kid—commit. You commit to something, you go strong, and everyone else will follow. He's playing like he can't decide what to have for lunch, let alone where to go when the pressure comes."

"Lions are tough this year, though," Bob's brother Joe put in. "Morehouse on the end." Joe was on the recliner, palming mixed nuts from a bowl on the arm.

"Morehouse, shit." Bob pulled the bottom of his shirt out from under the fold of belly above his belt. "Our line is letting him right by. I could get by these guys, a couple cups of coffee in me." Though six years older than Joe, and at least twenty-five pounds heavier, Bob still looked like his brother, sharing the same receding hairline and Reznik Roman nose.

It was Thanksgiving Day and Joe's wife Sue could be heard, even over the sounds of the television, in the kitchen lidding pots and opening and closing the oven. Their daughter Emily was seated at the set dining table talking on the phone. She was a gawky girl with glasses and thin hair pulled back into a ponytail. Bob rarely knew what to say to her. This was his first Thanksgiving since separating from Margaret, his first in two decades not spent at his own house. At least he was in Park Ridge, though, where he'd lived all his life, where he and Margaret raised Mike. For the past six months he'd been living in a place in Niles, the next town over. A perfectly decent place, all things considered, but not home. Disappointment and anger washed over him most nights as he strode up the stairs to his one-bedroom apartment.

Mike was a rookie. A runner up for the Heisman his senior year at Michigan, he was snatched up high in the second round of the draft. Through college he was constantly being compared to yesterday's stars, Marino and Montana. He broke two school records—passing yardage and touchdown passes—and was almost universally given credit for the crowd's attendance at games. Two straight sold-out seasons. People didn't come to see the team, they came to see him. They wore his jersey in the stands. They waited for the moment he lobbed a bomb, thirty-five, forty, fifty yards downfield. They came to see him chuck that thing between two defenders to his man cutting across the middle. They wanted to be fooled by his almost magical play action, their eyes following for a second the half-back gripping his imaginary ball, then realizing—*Wait!*—and readjusting on Mike just in time to see his arm let go a perfect toss, so fluid, to a man twenty yards down, on the sideline, right in the numbers.

The NFL, however, turned out to be a different game. Mike was brought in during a "rebuilding year." The team had lost six veterans the year before, three Pro Bowl-ers. Mike was to be the new anchor, the man to come in and helm a new passing game for what was to be a kind of finesse offense. But thus far in the season they had won only two games, against the Bears and the Seahawks, both sub-500 teams. The opinion among sportscasters, football pundits, and just about every Monday morning quarterback, was unanimous: Mike Reznik was a disappointment. All the trust and hope that had been put to him was lost a bit more with every sack, every incompletion, every fumbled snap.

Bob could feel the blood rushing through the veins in his neck. He finished the last of his Bud and cracked another open. The smell of turkey filled the first floor of the house. He had spent enough evenings the last two months here at Joe and Sue's house that the right side of the couch was his seat. If Emily was sitting there when Bob finished his dinner, she would move onto the floor or to the recliner or, as often as not, leave the room entirely. Bob paid little mind. His thoughts, when he was able to force them away from Margaret and the house, were wrapped up in Mike. He was the kid's coach back in the Peewee league days. He could, and often did, recall rustling up the kids, each in identical white helmet and blue jersey, for scrimmage. Most were unidentifiable, just marshmallow square torsos and snowman round heads, but he could always pick out Mike. Taller and leaner than most, Mike walked with a sort of prepubescent swagger, shoulders thrown back slightly, letting his feet lead the way. On the field, even in practice, he had an unending energy.

There was one game in particular that Bob remembered most. Not the whole game, really, but an incident. Mike was twelve, in his last season before high school, the last season Bob would be his coach, and he was playing left tackle on defense. It was the first half, early, no score, and Bob watched as his son took down the opposing team's quarterback. It was a clean one-on-one sack. Mike got up and looked to the ref who, for only a second, turned away. Bob saw his son, in that second, give a light tap of the toe of his cleat against the back of the quarterback's helmet. It of course should have been a penalty, and a costly one at that, but no one else saw it and so Bob said nothing. He knew he was supposed to give the speech, good sportsmanship and all that, but he also knew that this was a game where a strict adherence to the rules caused teams to lose.

—

Margaret Reznik stood staring out the sliding glass door at the browned remnants of her garden. All her plants were dead by then—the only evidences of their previous life were the hollowed twigs spiking out of the ground. She focused her sight closer, on her own reflection in the glass. Despite the softening of her skin, the wrinkles forming under her chin and around her temples, she was still an attractive woman on some level. She never had the knock-out features so coveted on supermarket magazine racks, was never the one men obsessed over, but there was a steadiness, a reliability to the way her brown eyes were set just-so above her relatively straight nose, the way her teeth formed an overbite behind her thin lips. She had the face of a wife, she thought: good-looking enough to marry, but not so beautiful as to instill insecurity or devotion in a husband.

She opened the door and stepped out onto the brick patio. The air was damp, and it smelled like snow, though it was still ten or so degrees too warm. She wandered farther into the yard, avoiding a patch of rabbit pellets that lay between the shriveled skeletons of two Inniswood hostas. Like her mother, Margaret preferred annuals in her garden. She knew why: because they were, by and large, nicer, prettier. Perennials were sturdy against the elements, providing shade in the summer and windbreaks in winter. But they incited no joy in her.

Margaret's mother, Noreen, slid open the door. "Mar?" Margaret turned, her arms crossed tightly across her chest. "They just scored another touchdown. You should come in and watch—maybe it'll bring Mikey some luck."

"I've got leaves in my gutters," Margaret said.

"Where?" Noreen asked, craning her neck toward the roof overhang.

"In the corner. I can see them, a big pile of them. Who cleans yours out?"

"Last year your brother was in town and he went up there."

"Well he can't come here every fall to clean out your gutters."

"I'm not asking him to. I'll pay someone, I guess," Noreen said.

The wind picked up and dislodged a lock of hair from behind Margaret's ear. She let her eyes move from the roof of her house to the trees looming above. She followed the line further, arching her back in a stiff ballerina pose, until she was millimeters from where she knew she'd topple off balance.

"Are you okay, honey?" Noreen asked.

She lurched forward. "I'm fine," she said lightly and joined her mother inside.

On the television, the Lions' seven-yard touchdown run was being shown in slow motion. The fullback took a wide pitch-out to the right side, a wall of blockers in front of him, and went strutting untouched into the end zone.

The Lions continue to march up and down the field with little or no resistance, the announcer said.

"Oh, I can't stand watching this," Margaret said. She leaned against the kitchen counter, unable to sit, her eyes set on the thirteen-inch TV fixed to the underside of the dish cabinet. Her mother was washing spinach in the sink, her sixty-seven-year-old fingers, pale and lined, moving the colander around under the rush of water. "It's those announcers," Margaret continued. "They're horrible. And all the graphics or whatever are just so silly, all machiney looking."

"Do you remember what your father used to do? During the Cubs' games? He would turn the sound down on the television and listen to the radio broadcast. He used to say that there were only two men in the world that he truly hated—Reagan and Harry Carey." She chuckled a short, nasally laugh and then became silent, the way she would whenever speaking about her husband, who died three years earlier. Despite the years, or maybe because of them, Margaret did not know what to do or say in these moments. She wanted to hug her mother, but the woman did not seem sad, exactly, only lost in thought. She liked, though, the fact that she had no idea what her mother was thinking, liked that she had thoughts and memories that belonged solely to herself.

"Are you going to call Dr. Rose?" Noreen asked, breaking the silence. Rose was a therapist Noreen had been seeing since a year after her husband's death.

"How do you know I haven't already?"

"Because I asked him."

"So much for doctor-patient confidentiality."

Noreen shut off the faucet and shook drops of water from the colander. "You have to be a patient first to enjoy that privilege, dear." She basted the turkey and replaced the makeshift tinfoil lid, tucking it around the bird with quick careful taps of her forefinger, and slid the rack, with some effort, back into the oven. "It might help you work on you," she said, "with everything going on."

"Don't you think that that's part of the problem though, Mom?" Margaret said with more force than intended. "Everyone's going around saying 'I have to think of me. I have to look out for myself. I need to work on my own identity.' And then all you have is however many billions of people, no one thinking about anyone but themselves, no one caring at all about—" she cut herself off. Her mother was looking at her, head cocked in such a way that Margaret felt like a child. It was amazing how she could still feel like a child.

The therapy conversation was all too familiar. Just after the announcement came that Mike was drafted, Margaret and Bob had been at the mall. After much debate about what to get their son as a congratulatory gift, they agreed upon a Raymond Weil Parsifal watch Margaret had seen at Macy's. Making their way through the crowds, Bob marching two paces ahead, Margaret trotted in order to keep up. The crowd seemed to part for Bob; shoppers with their purses and shopping bags and baby strollers veered right or left as if the last thing they would want to do was to impede his progress. Behind him, though, the sea of people rushed back together, jostling and tripping Margaret who was dancing sideways to make herself less. Passing a Victoria's Secret, she saw Bob slow his pace, almost imperceptibly, and turn his head. She could not tell exactly what he was looking at—a variety of bras, panties, and negligees decorated the mannequins in the window—and it could have been that he was looking at the lingerie in a general man way, or that he was simply admiring the impossible forms of the dummies, but she was convinced, at that moment, that he was having an affair. He was window-shopping for a gift. She'd had the feeling before: mysterious nights out with "the guys from work," the times he'd send Mike home from practice with other parents so he could stay and work on the playbook. This time was different, though. She knew. No hard evidence, of course, but it was a fact. Call it intuition. Call it extra sensory perceptions.

At the watch counter, the saleswoman was busied with another customer, a tall man, early thirties, buying a woman's Cartier. Bob drummed his fingers on the glass while peering in at the men's selection.

"Who is she?" Margaret asked in a whisper. Bob did not look up. "No, I don't care. I just want you to tell me the truth. Just tell me so I know."

"What the hell are you talking about?" he responded, equally hushed.

"Just tell me." She was not upset. She was confused, profoundly so, and within that confusion there was little room for any kind of definite emotion. Everything was whirling, being tossed around between the walls of her mind and heart.

Bob raised his eyes to the wall behind the counter and let out a snort of a laugh. "You're paranoid." Paranoia—this was what Bob called it. "You need to see someone, a professional." He took a credit card from his wallet and tossed it onto the glass case. "Put the thing on this. I'll meet you at the car." He walked away toward the mall entrance, tucking his wallet back into his pocket.

If they talked infrequently and without depth before that day, then what followed was an outright disdainful silence.

—

Bob had cheated. With three different women over the last fifteen years, he had ongoing relationships. With several others he had nights of nameless, faceless fucking. The first relationship was with the mother of a teammate of Mike's in Peewee. Sandy Filmore was a cartoon of herself: bored housewife with too much time who took to following her lone child, doting. She was at a practice, standing on a patch of grass halfway between the football field and her car. It was still hot then, early September, and she wore an orange tank-top which accentuated the freckles on her face, neck, and chest, and an unflattering pair of white pleated shorts which bulged out at the sides, making her wide hips appear even wider. Bob spotted her and waved her over. He had no intentions at that point beyond what he thought to be harmless flirting. He would act in a gregarious manner, teetering on the edge of obnoxious without actually plunging over the side, until he got her to laugh and touch his arm lightly with her fingers. He loved that. He had always enjoyed the attention of women and, though he had never—not since being married anyway— sought it out, he welcomed it. Sandy was a cinch.

"Which one of these midgets is yours?" he asked, when she was close enough for words.

"Kevin Filmore."

Kevin, he knew, was new to the area, having moved from a south suburb that summer.

"Up here from—where was it? Berwyn?"

"That's right," she said, seeming impressed by his knowledge of her family's recent history.

"Well, you gotta get used to things here on the North side. Our summer is your winter." It took a moment, but eventually she smiled, having gotten the joke. "Bob Reznik," he said, extending a hand.

Over the next few months the two of them got to know

each other in between scrimmages and while the kids ran drills. When the season officially began, Bob would see Sandy in the stands, shivering now in the autumn wind. Her husband Ed was there too and she would sneak waves to Bob while Ed was shouting harsh words of encouragement to little Kevin. It was actually Sandy who did the propositioning one windy afternoon late in the season. There was something she wanted to talk to him about. Could he meet her for coffee that Friday? He went to the Perkins restaurant and found Sandy more dolled-up than usual: lipstick, perfume, painted nails. She was drinking a tall glass of iced tea as he walked up to the table. The soft, cream-colored sweater showed off an ample bosom and Bob wondered why it was that in the early days of practice, the days of T-shirts, he hadn't noticed how generously proportioned she was. His question was answered an hour later as he was removing her padded satin brassiere.

He wanted to think, looking back on this moment as he often did, that he had no intention of doing it again, that it was a mistake from which he'd learn. But that wasn't true. He knew he would do it again. And again. He liked it. Not just the physical part; what was more satisfying was the feeling that Sandy wanted him, and the knowledge that, if he wanted to, he could make her need him.

Their affair lasted three months, though now Bob could not remember exactly how many times they met, how many afternoons and early evenings he spent in her bed moaning and grunting like a sick animal, like he never did with Margaret. When Sandy told him, one day at practice, that she thought Ed was getting suspicious, Bob cut her off.

"I think it might be that this thing has run its course," he said.

"Well, we don't have to make any rash decisions here," she responded nervously. "I just think we need to be extra careful."

"It's not just Ed," he said, seeming to examine the roster list on his clipboard. "I just think maybe it's done, that's all."

He could feel her looking at him, staring confused and pleading. After a minute, Sandy turned and walked back to her car. He knew at that moment that he would miss being with her. He would miss the taste of her skin and the weight of her breast in his hand, the feel of her hair dragging down his chest, the way she would grip his ass with her hand when she was almost there. But he would also miss her at practice, the light conversations they'd had about kids or movies or nothing at all. He realized that she was a friend, something he hadn't had in a while. But he knew that they would have to end eventually—Ed would find out or, worse, Margaret—and he would not let her be the one to say the words. He would not be the one to lose.

The other relationships were longer, each about six months, but the women—a co-worker from another department and a younger one, at least ten years Bob's junior, who he met waiting to get his oil changed—meant little to him aside from the physical pleasure they brought him. They were both attractive and funny in their ways, but the excitement was in the act, not in the participants. He ended those too at the first sign of a dying wind.

—

The thing that Margaret wanted to remember was the house, and Bob and Mike pulling up in Bob's wagon just ahead of her. She could see the back of Bob's head clearly outlined in silhouette, but Mike was in his usual slumped pose and only the very peak of his head was visible above the headrest. Normally, they would tumble out of the car, Mike first racing to the door, and Bob tiredly lumbering behind, fumbling with his keys, but this once they stayed in the car for a minute. It was evening and the sky was purplish and still. She had just gotten home from the office. From one car into the other, she saw Bob turn to the right, his head tilted down slightly. His arms were out in front of him, as if he were adjusting Mike's hat or fixing his hair. Margaret walked to the other car and Mike's door flew open. She saw on his forehead a square of gauze bandage taped down. In his light blond hair were streaks of pink starting at his temple and disappearing behind his ear.

"Don't freak out, Mom," Mike said, Bob's attitude in the words and voice of a twelve-year-old. Bob got out on the other side.

"What happened?"

"Toby ran into me while I was on the sidelines and his helmet cut me."

"Five stitches," Bob said. "No big deal."

Minutes later, Mike was up in his room, and Margaret and Bob in the kitchen.

"You didn't try to call me?"

"I told you, it was nothing. A couple stitches."

"Stitches aren't nothing, Bob. Stitches are very much something. Jesus, I can't believe you'd be at the hospital with our son and you didn't call."

"What were you going to do? Come and assist the doctor?"

"Not the point," she said through gritted teeth, trying her best to keep from screaming. "Did you think maybe he would have wanted me there?"

"Yeah, that's what a kid wants, his mother standing over him blubbering."

"I had a right to be there," she shrieked, her voice echoing through the room.

She was silent through dinner.

"Everyone was old." Mike talked about the emergency room as if it were part of a school field trip. The Museum of

Natural History. "There was this old lady who was missing an eye—she didn't have a patch over it or anything, it was just this big, wrinkly hole. It was so gross. Everyone had canes or wheelchairs or something. This one old guy had a bloody nose and he had to keep his head back and he was like that the whole time we were there. I'll bet his neck started to hurt. I'll bet my blood is still on Toby's helmet."

Bob laughed.

Margaret wanted to remember this. Bob's open mouth, laughing. Their matching china cabinets behind him, framing him, the chandelier she'd installed lighting his face. The rooms of this house were the scene of his cruelty and she needed them. She wanted her anger to be whole and uninterrupted.

What she did not want to remember was when she and Bob were first married, before Mike. When they drove downstate in the old Charger to visit a cypress forest they had read about in the travel section of the paper. Fourteen thousand acres of drooping, moss covered cypress trees. The mist across the area veiled anything more than twenty feet out and gave the place an otherworldly feel, like something out of a fantasy novel. A wooden walkway meandered through the forest, two feet above the soaked, swampy ground. They walked these planks all day until their legs burned and their arms felt heavy like wet fabric. They spent the two nights they were there eating pot roast specials and pie a la mode at a tiny diner and drinking cold, cheap beer at a local bar, Don McLean and the Allman Brothers in heavy rotation on the juke. In the rented cabin, they made love while the television flickered the fuzzy nightly news.

And she did not want to let herself think about the last six months, the numbness in which she lived. The two of them eating different meals in different rooms. Her sitting in the dining room reading the paper while Bob watched the sports recap in the basement. The light changing through the house as night took control from dusk. The silence was only broken for the last two minutes of their marriage. It was a Saturday and they crossed paths in the living room. They passed each other, but both stopped and turned.

"This is ridiculous," Margaret said. "Do you want to leave or should I?"

Bob did not move, did not even blink, for ten or so seconds.

"I'll go pack some things," he replied finally.

He made several trips up and down the stairs, and out to his car. What he had in the bags and boxes was a mystery that she cared little about; he could have it all, if he wanted. There were few things she required: a chair, books, a roof. She would have been the one to leave, but as he shut the door and walked to his car (no goodbye; not so much as a glance to acknowledge the years) she was happy to still have her garden to keep her busy.

She tended to it. She took two days off from work and clipped, raked, and watered her way from one end of the yard to the other. A trellis placed too close to the wall was allowing vine to attach itself to the brick and Margaret spent an afternoon doing her best to prune and redirect. Many of her bulbs—the yellow and white tulips that bordered the garage and side of the house, the lilies and buttercups circling the sundial—had already expired, but the impatiens and verbena were still bright and strong. She mowed the lawn in a diagonal, the way Bob always had; for years she had never known why he did it this way until one day she noticed a baseball outfield—Fenway maybe—on the TV. She continued her own yard in the same lines, afraid that if she changed it, tried to go straight across, she might end up with some sort of argyle design. At night, from her usual seat at the dining table, she would glance out the glass of the door and watch the moths gathering and bumping stupidly against each other in the cone of light from a flood lamp.

After three days, the phone rang. Margaret jogged in, tossing her muddy gloves onto the patio. "I want the house," Bob said. His voice was business-like. "I thought about it and I want the house."

—

It was midway through the fourth quarter. Mike had completed three solid passes in a row to set up a seven-yard run into the end zone, but the Lions countered on their next possession, making the score 28–13. It would be one of the great comebacks if Mike could pull it off. Bob was not holding his breath.

"I don't need this right now, you know that," he said, apparently to Joe, but really to no one. He got up and paced the room. "I should be sitting here watching that boy win. I spent enough time out there with him." He set his can down, ignoring the Impressionist painters coasters scattered here and there on the table. "I'll tell you where I should be: I should be in my own goddamn house watching him win this fucking game."

"Easy," Joe said.

Bob looked over to Emily, who was now peering up from a magazine. They made eye contact for a second before she turned away. "What are you reading there, Em?" he asked. Joe's eyes moved back and forth between them, unsettled.

"A magazine."

"It good?"

She shrugged. Bob sat down at the table across from her. "What do you got?" He laid a hand down on the pages of the magazine and spun it around. *Get Your Crush and Keep Him!* was written in slanted, imitation chalk-on-blackboard script across the top. The article seemed to be a step-by-step guide to pubescent love. He read out loud, "Step one: Be yourself." He slammed his hand down on the table. "Nothing wrong with that advice," he said. "Pretty girl like you shouldn't have to have to put on a show for anyone."

"Mom," Emily said past Bob's head to where her mother was in the kitchen. Bob looked over his shoulder just as Sue was waving a hand and furrowing her brow. He turned back and put up a hand of peace right in his niece's line of vision.

"No kidding, I would do anything to be in your shoes. You can do whatever you want. But once you get older, watch out—you get stuck," he pointed a finger at her, "and there's nothing you can do once you're stuck. Just wave your arms around, trying to breathe. Listen to me here, I know what I'm talking about. This is stuff you're gonna have to go through, so do yourself a favor and take a lesson from me."

"Bob," Sue said, "she's thirteen."

"Bob!" Joe yelled from the recliner chair. "Come on, we're taking it down the field."

He ignored his name and kept looking straight at Emily. Her eyes were a similar brown to his, he noticed for the first time. Both Sue and Joe said his name again. He knew she did not like him, or was afraid of him, but despite this and her parents' calls, she held his gaze—God bless her—with a hardheaded stubbornness he respected. Perhaps there was someone in the family he was true kin with, someone with whom he had more in common than just a name.

—

Happy Thanksgiving, Mom and Dad. I wish I could be there, but I'm a little busy right now. Mike's face filled the screen, white teeth like blank dominoes between his lips. His image shrank and whooshed away, revealing a different view of Margaret's son: standing on the sideline, helmet propped on top of his head, being yelled at by his coach. The old man repeatedly poked at a clipboard in his hand and then pointed at Mike.

He's not smiling anymore, Pat said.

That video obviously recorded before this debacle began, Bill added with a lilt of amusement in his voice.

Dinner was just about ready—the turkey a crisp gold-brown, the gravy bubbling, the carrots soft and buttered—when the two-minute warning stopped play. Margaret wiped a tear from below her eye before it could progress down the length of her face, before her mother could notice. She went to the front door and stepped out onto the porch. The air smelled like nothing—no food or flowers—and she breathed it in. Cars lined the street. The outside furniture cushions had been brought in for the year. She sat on the cold checkerboard metal of a chair and tried to remember how many sets of porch furniture they had gone through in the years in the house. The first set rusted, or maybe that was the second. Mike and a friend broke a rocking love seat with one ambitious tackle. There were others, though.

A blue Mazda sedan pulled up and parallel-parked two houses down, between a matching set of mini-vans. A man, probably in his fifties, emerged. His build was slight, fragile even, and he sported a gray mustache over his lip. The collar of an Oxford shirt peeked out from the top of his blue sweater. The same blue as his car. Leaning into the backseat, he took out a casserole dish covered with tin foil. Margaret looked away, but could still see the man, out of the corner of her eye, coming up the walk of Roger and Nicole Nelson's house next door. She pretended to be watching the line where the sky met the treetops of the forest preserve down the road. The sun was low and hidden behind the clouds. The man hesitated on the steps, now outside of her periphery.

"Escaping?" His voice was as wiry as his body. Margaret looked over with a jerk of her neck.

"No," she said quickly.

"Oh," the man said. "The holidays, though, they get to be a bit much. I just thought…"

"Mmm, no, I'm fine."

He stood for another second, then lifted the dish up to his chest as a sort of salute. "Well. Happy Thanksgiving. Gotta catch the end of the game."

"That's my son," she said suddenly. "He's the—"

"Oh, that's you. Or him. Nicole told me one of her neighbors' son was Mike Reznik. You must be proud."

"I am." She stood up.

"Nervous?"

"About what?"

"I'd just think it would be pretty nerve-wracking having a kid in that kind of profession. Satisfying, too, but still. Pretty nerve-wracking."

"It is," she said matter-of-factly. "Sometimes I wish he had gone into banking. Or better yet became an artist—you know, something where failure was the norm." She stopped. "What a terrible thing to say."

"No—"

"I just mean…yes, it's hard."

"Yeah," he said understandingly. A car passed by slowly, a young women in the driver's seat hunched over, peering out the passenger window. The man caught sight of this and smiled. The woman waved and lurched forward to an open spot of curb. "My daughter," the man said to Margaret.

"I need to get back to dinner," she said.

"Okay. Well, I'll be rooting for Mike. It was nice—"

"Yeah, you too." She fumbled at the doorknob and, finally getting it open, went inside. Her mother was fluffing the flower centerpiece on the table. There was something charming about the way the man smiled at the sight of his daughter. He wasn't her type—if it could be said that she had a type. When she used to date, she always went for bigger men, thick through the shoulders. Her boyfriend before Bob, the man she was dating when she met Bob, in fact, was bookish and uncoordinated, but large enough to give the impression of athleticism. With a broad chest and large hands, he could have been a defensive end or a shotputter instead of a chemistry major. They dated for three months before sleeping together, and when they did it was purely missionary and less than satisfying. She broke up with him to date Bob, who she slept with on their second date. "I want you," he had said quietly into her ear and she gave herself.

At the side of the front window, angling herself to peer around the curtains, Margaret watched the man's daughter come up to the Nelson's house. She could hear the carriage horse sound of the young woman's high heels on the sidewalk. The man went back down the stairs to meet her and, still holding the casserole dish, gave her a one-armed hug. From Margaret's position, because of the dim, ethereal light outside, the two of them were almost completely in silhouette. It reminded her of a dream she had years before where she was surrounded by empty, black forms. She knew each of them by name—Bob, Mike, Mom—but she also knew that they were not them, exactly, but their absence, like a vacuum. Each form was a void, each movement a lack of movement. They moved around and past her, almost touching her, and she had to constantly dodge them. Contact would transform her, make her too disappear. This seemed to go on all night, her ducking and spinning to avoid them, and when she woke she found the other side of the bed empty. It was early morning, not yet five, and she was still trying to make sense of consciousness. Bob emerged from the bathroom and got back into bed without noticing that his wife was awake. Margaret found it to be something that he was gone when she woke from this dream—not exactly ironic or telling, but something. Perhaps appropriate.

The man and his daughter disappeared into the house. Margaret leaned her forehead into the curtains.

"Hungry?" Noreen asked from the kitchen.

"Not really," Margaret answered with an exhale of breath that could have been mistaken for a laugh.

"You will be."

Together they lifted the bird from the oven, set it on the stove, and transferred it to a yellow ceramic serving platter. Margaret began scooping the stuffing into a bowl. On the television, a time out had been taken and now Santa was selling computers while an elf played the fool, his squat frame comically crushed under a red bag of goodies. Margaret tried to think of what she would say to Mike when he called later. You weren't getting any protection. The refs were blind. You'll get 'em next week. I love you.

"You could get a private detective," Noreen said.

"Mom," Margaret pleaded.

"Well, you could. That's all I'm saying. Prove he cheated."

"And how is someone going to do that?"

"If I knew how, we wouldn't have to hire someone." She stopped talking just long enough for Margaret to think the subject was done. Both women switched stations as if choreographed—Margaret on to rolls, Noreen to the salad. "But if you did," she continued, slicing a knife through a cucumber, "then the judge would have to give you the house."

"He might anyway."

"I don't like all this fifty-fifty business your man is giving you. We should be able to get better chances than that. I mean, what are you paying him for? Bob wasn't exactly true, and everyone knows it."

"That doesn't matter," Margaret said. "None of it matters."

"It matters if you want to keep the house. You cannot let that man win. You can't lay down and let him take your home."

"It's not much of a home nowadays, Mom."

—

Bob and Joe stood in the garage, smoking cigarettes. There was an old coffee can on the floor of the garage for their butts. The room was damp and smelled like ashes and rust. Bob lit his cigarette and tossed the match, missing the can just barely. The shelves that lined each of the three walls were piled with tools, empty flowerpots, and boxes marked *X-mas* and *Fragile* and *Sewing Stuff*. Set atop the rafters above their heads was a canoe and several fishing rods. Bob had not heard of his brother fishing in years, and canoeing never. His eyes met all of these objects with a glaring, wholehearted disdain. At the center of it all was Sue's Camry, silver and clean as the day it was bought. Bob had been out here hundreds of times before, but it never seemed as pathetic as it did then. This was where Joe was sent to smoke: not inside, not out in the front or backyard. Surrounded by junk, most of which was not his. And there he was, standing blankly beside his wife's nicer-than-his car.

"The girls are making me go out to the mall in the morning," Joe said. "What do they call it, door-busting? Don't suppose you want to come."

"No chance," Bob said.

The last time he was at a mall was the watch day. Margaret knew he cheated, though, ironically, he hadn't been at the time. It had been a while, in fact, over a year. Not for lack of trying. Bob found himself these days seeking women out, sizing them up at bars or the grocery store, his tastes becoming more indefinite, encompassing just about anyone willing. Regardless of age or even relative beauty, they were all just chances to score. He didn't care who they were, what they did for a living, whether or not they were attached. All he wanted was to be on top of them, and for them to want him. He wanted them to ask for more and he wanted to leave them there.

Bob went to the car.

"Is this open?" he asked as he pulled the handle of the driver's side door and the rubber seals puckered apart.

"Hey, don't," Joe said. "It's gonna get all smoky."

"I just need to use the ashtray," Bob said, sitting in the driver's seat, his feet still on the garage floor.

"Don't use the goddamn ashtray in there, use the can, what's wrong with you?"

Bob stood and shut the car door. Joe let out an audible breath and shook his head. "Like Margaret let you smoke in her car," he said. It was the first time in weeks her name had been spoken aloud between them. Joe batted at the red string hanging from the automatic door opener, the one Bob helped install a year before. "Have you talked to her?" he asked weakly. Bob made no answer, only thumped a thumb against the roof of the car. "Are you still going after the house?"

"Why shouldn't I?" Bob said. "This was her idea. She said the words."

"Come on, Bob."

"Come on, what?"

"You know."

"She's got nothing on me. What can she say, 'I think he did this or that'? She doesn't know anything."

"She knows everything. Not specifics, but still."

"She can't prove it."

"That doesn't mean she's not right."

"Right doesn't mean shit," Bob said. "The only things

that matter are what you have, what you want, and going after it."

"Save me the halftime speech, coach."

"You don't know anything, you know. You got your little wife here. Your kid. You think everything is all fine." He rubbed the back of his head. "You don't know how it is."

"How what—"

"Tell me how to deal with my life," he said to himself, then, "You got it easy, you know that. Look at you."

Joe stubbed the cherry of his cigarette against the inside of the can, orange embers falling and disappearing, and dropped the butt. "I'm not listening to this," he said, and went through the door, back into the kitchen.

Left to himself, Bob leaned against the car and brought the tip of his cigarette to within centimeters of the paint job. He wondered how hot it would have to be before the paint began to blister and peel. Hotter than a cigarette certainly. He took a basketball down from one of the shelves and bounced slowly and rhythmically, enjoying the rubbery echo through the garage and the knowledge that the sound was extending to the inside of the house. He held the ball and cocked his arm back in throwing position. He could destroy the shelf with the flowerpots in one motion. He dropped the ball.

Inside, on the TV, the Lions were kneeling on the snap. The clock was ticking down, 1:03, 1:02, and the crowd was cheering wildly. The players on the Lions' sidelines were laughing and slapping hands, looking directly into the camera, holding up single fingers of victory. The coach was trying to remain serious, as if the game were still up for grabs, but broke down into a smile when an assistant said something close to his ear. The camera then angled on the opposite sideline, panning sullen and exhausted faces. Mike was in a cap now, his helmet discarded, his arms crossed across his number. With twelve seconds still on the clock, both sides took over the field, meeting in the middle. The coaches shook hands and slapped each other's shoulders and exchanged quick words. Mike shook with the Lions' quarterback and left the field.

"We got the Eagles next week," Joe said. "We can take them."

Bob was standing behind him and hadn't known whether or not his brother was aware of his presence. He stepped across the room and took his jacket from the closet.

"I'm going," he said.

"Where are you going?"

"Home."

"You can't drive, Bob. You had too much to drink."

"I'm going," he said again.

"What are you going to do? Sit in the apartment by yourself on Thanksgiving?"

"I'm not going to the apartment. I'm going home." He knew Emily was behind him, watching as he spoke. Peering up from her teen nothing rag. Her dull brown eyes sucking in the little light there was.

"You're being a child," Sue said.

"Children are so pure," Bob said ironically, his arms gliding past the dry cotton of his jacket's sleeves.

—

Margaret wanted to jump through the window. She turned her head periodically, catching view of the Nelsons' house behind her. The squared window reflection was caught in her mother's eyeglasses. She could see no movement, but every once in a while an explosion of voices or laughter would burst through the silence. The television in the kitchen was now dark; the food—far too much for just her and Noreen—was spread across the table, picturesque. No Grace was said, the meal instead christened by a clink of bulbous red wine glasses.

"For all we have," Noreen said ceremoniously.

"All we have," Margaret repeated, trying hard to believe it.

They went through the mechanics of mealtime: asking and passing and chewing. Noreen relayed information she had read in an article about holiday traditions at homeless shelters: over fifty turkeys had been donated to one shelter the year before and they had to turn away would-be volunteers.

"They could have gone back and helped the next week, but how many do you think actually did?"

"Two?"

"I don't know," Noreen said. "What I'm saying is that people need help all the time, not just on these certain days. These volunteers, I suspect, are only trying to make themselves feel better about taking more than their share of the pot."

"What about those people who do nothing?"

"Well, that's not good either, but at least they're not using an empty gesture to avoid their own reality."

Margaret normally loved these conversations with her mother. She was full of surprises. They could be talking about anything, a shade of paint on a house, and she could suddenly become so eloquent, relating the topic to a larger world. But now Margaret only wanted silence. She did not want to feel guilty for her pain. She did not want a voice of reason. She wanted what was next door, whatever it was. Her desire at that moment was to be split in two: one side drunk and oblivious and the other remembering and harboring. She wanted to be asleep in bed while driving far away from anything she knew.

No. What she wanted was this: a moment eight years before, when Mike was fifteen. It was a Friday night in the fall and Bob was out of town. She had fallen asleep on the couch, a magazine splayed on her chest. Around midnight she was woken by the creek of the front door. She must have, at some point she did not remember, turned off the light above her. Through the darkness of the room and the blur of sleep she saw Mike carefully latch the door shut and set the chain in place—it took him three tries to get it. Holding on to the half wall next to him, he maneuvered out of the entryway and into the room proper. Three steps in, his leg hit the ottoman and he fell forward, one hand on the floor. Margaret knew the situation, though she had not before had to deal with it and she was surprised that it had come so early, but still she could not help but laugh to herself at the thought that entered her mind: I have given birth to Dick Van Dyke. If it weren't for this thought she might have been angry, might have yelled *How dare you* or *Wait until your father finds out*. Instead, she simply lifted herself up onto an elbow. Mike stood up halfway and gasped, startled. He swayed just slightly.

"I didn't see you," he said.

"I fell asleep."

"We won," he said. It was his first year on Varsity.

"I might have guessed," she said. "I'm glad." She stood and walked to the stairs. "Don't make a habit of this." He was staring at his feet. She started up the stairs. "Drink some water before you go to bed."

She never told Bob or anyone about this. She was not mad, nor did she feel any sort of maternal disappointment. She went to sleep that night with a great feeling of contentment. Remaining on her side of the bed, the sheets slowly collecting warmth from her body, she held the satisfaction of a shared secret. More than any other time she could think of, she felt like she and her son were family.

—

Joe drove. After ten minutes of back and forth arguing, he had agreed to take Bob to his house.

"For only a minute, Bob," he had said, "and then we're coming back here for our goddamn Thanksgiving dinner." The house was twenty minutes from Joe and Sue's. They were one of only a few cars on the road and as they left the residential neighborhoods and got onto Oakton Street, the main road that bisected the suburbs east and west, Bob did his best to empty his mind of thoughts of action and motivation. He did not know why he was going or what he would do once he got there. He only knew that he was on his way and that he had started this.

He expected a rush of feeling to enter him at sight of the house, a feeling of righteousness or belonging. Something. But as they passed it and pulled into an open spot down the street, he felt nothing good in him. The Lions' players and coach were being interviewed on the radio when Joe cut the engine. The street looked the same, and he had to remind himself that he had only been gone two months. It seemed longer, a year at least. He flung the car door open and sprung out, but this was forced; his energy was gone. He walked forward anyway, his shoulders slumped slightly forward leading the way.

"Five minutes, Bob," Joe said, shutting his door and following. "I don't even know what we're doing here, but I'm serious. Five minutes."

Bob ignored him and kept going. In his head he began recreating a meeting he'd had with his lawyer a month before. She had no proof of wrongdoing, the lawyer said. As long as he behaved himself, she'd be in for a long fight. Bob knew Margaret couldn't fight, that she would give up and the house would be his. He didn't want it. Options flashed in his mind, but he knew that there only one. He could not quit; he would have to lose.

He still had keys. The lights were on, but stepping up to the porch he could not hear anything from inside. The furniture cushions were gone, as was Bob's ashtray. He wondered, as he pulled the key chain from his pocket, if Margaret had changed the lock. She hadn't. The key went in smoothly and turned with ease. Margaret was walking into the living room, towards the door, as he stepped inside. She was holding a cloth napkin in her hand. Her mother was just behind. Bob stepped in followed by Joe. They were all still, not speaking, barely breathing. Every word Bob knew was exploding in his head, every feeling trying to explain its way to understanding and control. He dropped his head and took three steps forward. Margaret stood still as a picture in front of him. Hair, eyes, mouth, neck, shoulders—everything was her, right there.

Such a simple motion. His hand flew up and connected, open palm, with her cheek. The sound was not a sharp smack, but dull like a limp balloon being popped. She fell back into an end table. Her hair swung across her face. The lamp knocked against the wall and went out. Noreen let out a curt yelp. Joe had Bob from behind, his arms wrapped around him in a bear hug, and was tugging him backwards in short, jerking movements. Noreen and Joe, they were witnesses. This Bob knew. They would stand before the judge and describe this act and his decision would be simple, easy. In the light left over from the dining room, Bob watched Noreen's frail hands lightly holding either side of her daughter's face. Joe was saying something, cursing. Bob's words were still stuck in his head as he watched Margaret stand, but had now formed into two perfect utterances: *This is your house* and *I'm sorry*. He repeated the latter over and over as he was pushed out the door.

—

The door slammed shut and Margaret sat on the couch. She breathed in slowly, trying to settle her heart. The spot where Bob's hand hit her face felt like it was covered with hot spiders. She put the back of her hand to it and it cooled slightly, but the tingling was still there. She had never been hit before and was surprised how direct it was—nothing between you and the sensation. Her mind was shaken.

Noreen began to speak, but Margaret put her hand up to stop her. Silence covered the house. The air itself seemed to pause even its most subtle movement. Her eyes took in the room. It was a still life: the chairs and tables, the front door, a ceramic turkey on the half wall, the picture window with its frozen world outside, her mother. Margaret was a part of it. Her hands on her knees, the tip of her nose. It had all grown there, come up from the ground out of nothing with undetectable slowness.

Suddenly she got up and tucked her hair behind her ears. Noreen was watching, her eyes wide and mouth ajar, and Margaret recognized the expression on her face as fear.

"It's all so silly," Margaret said just before the phone rang.

Everybody's Irish

Out on the curb, you deposit a small box of paperbacks next to the rest of the items not worth putting in storage: a wobbly card table, a busted file cabinet, old CDs and video tapes, out-of-fashion shorts and neckties, hangers, pots and pans, a bag of clothes Maeve and Franny have long outgrown. Passers-by glance down at what you've discarded. Upstairs, the apartment where you've lived for the past seven years, since just before Maeve was born, is empty and cleaner than it has ever been. You've made sure of this. No one is going to look around and say your family was a bunch of bums.

You bring the last box—a shoebox jammed with papers and a toothbrush and other miscellanea you may need handy—to your Corolla and slip it into a tight space beneath the passenger seat. The back and trunk are jammed with more boxes and bags of clothes. You sit a moment in the driver's seat and figure your wife and daughters are probably to Champaign by now. By tomorrow night, barring anything unforeseen, they should be in Houston, at Sally's folks' place, where the girls will climb the stairs and flop down on beds in spare rooms kept immaculate for visits of pleasure or, in this case, necessity.

Breathing becomes difficult in the cramped car, a choking sensation rising from your lungs to the tender base of your throat, so you get out, walk down the street and go into a bar you've passed a thousand times but never entered. You don't generally like bars. You're not a big drinker. But you settle onto a stool and order a Sprite, mentally calculating what such a simple thing might cost here, and how much you are expected to tip.

A current of cold air hits you in the back and a group of four men enter. Three take a table and one sidles next to you and raps his knuckles on the polished wood of the bar. "Hell of a day out there," he says to no one in particular. He orders a round of beers, then says, "Seen the river?"

"Sorry?" you say. On his chest is affixed a nametag printed with the words *Mitchell Information Networks,* and, below that, written in Sharpie, *Carter.*

"It's green today, isn't it?"

"Thing's green every day," you say.

"But not like today, right?" The bartender brings his drinks and Carter pays and gives you a jovial wink before disappearing backwards.

In your mind, you replay the moments, just hours ago, when your girls left. You kissed Maeve and Franny through the backseat windows, but the driver's side was open only a crack, and you wonder if you missed your last chance to kiss your wife.

Twenty minutes later, Carter is back. "This city is a party today," he says. Carter introduces himself and you reciprocate. "What's your line of work, friend?" he asks.

"Are we going to talk work at a party, Carter?" you say, and this amuses him. He smiles and slaps you on the back.

"Absolutely right," he said. He points at your glass.

"You're on empty. What's it: gin and tonic? Vodka tonic?"

You lie and say, "Gin." Carter adds a gin and tonic to the bartender's work order. He glances out the window and says, "I'm telling you, it is a party out there in this goddamn city."

—

"Kids?" the man next to you at the table asks. His nametag says *Fisk* and he's a doughy, friendly-seeming guy about your age. "You got kids?"

"Two girls," you say. "Six and four."

"Three here. Two boys and a girl. Twelve, ten, and seven. Where's the little lady today?"

You look at the digital clock on the wall but can't get any information from it. After a half-second, you realize it isn't a clock at all but an advertisement for Guinness, a countdown to St. Patrick's Day reading 00:00:00:00. You look at your watch. "Carbondale," you say to Fisk.

"Separated?" he asks, his mouth pursed.

"No," you say with more force than intended. What you and Sally are has not been defined. As losing the apartment became more and more inevitable, you both took on a resigned wait-and-see approach to the future. "We'll just see what happens," she said, and you wondered at what point you would look at the present and say, *This happened.* The state of your marriage, your relationship with your daughters, the very place where you will sleep tonight: all of it is unclear. This happened. The only reason you are still in the city is that last week you hit upon two leads on gigs, one flying one with a regional commuter service, the other taking skydivers over the cornfields west of the suburbs. This is your profession. You are a pilot. Neither job is sure by any means—you know too many guys grounded for lack of work—but you and Sally agreed that you should follow until the trail went cold. You even feigned optimism and told the girls that they were simply taking a vacation to their grandparents' and that they would come home in a couple weeks to a brand new apartment. They did their best to sound excited about it all, which smashed your heart apart.

"Just visiting then? Carbondale?"

"Just visiting," you say.

"I think I was there once," Fisk says. "Carbondale? On a contract job. We do computers, but you probably already know that?"

All you know about these men is that they invited you to sit down, and now that they "do computers," whatever that means.

You accept another drink from Carter, but your palms sweat at the prospect of having to get a round yourself. Then, as if reading your mind, Carter bellows across the table, "Don't worry about it, friend. It's on the company. Per diem. More than we can drink ourselves. You're doing us a favor, 'cause I'm spending every goddamn dime they allow."

"Are they picking everything up?" Fisk asks.

"Hey," Carter says with authority, pointing a finger at his colleague. "Fuck Mancinelli and the rest of the brass."

"Easy down, gents," the bartender calls to the table in a phony lilting brogue. "The day of St. Patrick doesn't call for such execration." But by the look he gives right after, you know he isn't entirely joking.

"We're in from Cincinnati," Fisk says, leaning into you. "But all our big execs are based here or New York. They brought us in to try and grab clients at the convention? At McCormick Place? Didn't really work out so well."

"Fucking waste of time," a big, broad man whose nametag reads *Winarski* says. His voice is so deep it seems to echo itself. Groups of people stream in to the bar, beautiful kids in their twenties all dressed in green, clovers on their cheeks like lipstick smacks. They gather near the table, where the name-tagged men down two drinks to your one, and then do it again. More people come in, and a guy in a striped rugby shirt bumps into Winarski's chair with his hip.

"Do you mind?" Winarski says.

"Where do you want me to go?" the guy says, gesturing to the crowd.

"Are you actually asking?" Winarski says.

"Relax," the guy says.

"The river is the thing today," Carter says. You don't know if he's trying to diffuse a situation or if he's just fixated. "The Chicago River on Saint Patrick's Day. This is a thing a man has to see. Am I right?" The rest of the men say nothing. "Good Christ, you men are about as enthusiastic as a box of turds."

"The river?" Fisk says.

"We get up from this table, get a cab, and emerge at the green Chicago River. Let's go!" Carter bangs a fist on the table, clattering bottles and glasses together. "Let's go!" he yells again.

"Come on, guys," the bartender calls. "Take it easy." No brogue this time.

Carter ignores him. "Let's go!" he hollers, banging on the table. "Let's go!"

"Go then," someone from the crowd says.

"Alright," the bartender says.

—

Out on the street, having been asked to leave the bar, Carter tosses an arm around your shoulder, says, "You're coming with us, yes?"

Here is a choice you'd like to take a moment with. A second to orient yourself. But all you have time to weigh is solitude on one hand and distraction on the other. "Yes," you say.

"There we go," he says.

The group wanders southward and passes your parked Corolla. Winarski raps on the window distractedly. "What goes on here?" he says.

Your belongings are pressed up against the glass.

"Bad luck or bad habits," Carter says.

"My money's on habits," Winarski says. "Make your own luck."

What kind of luck have you made? You worked every angle you could think of with every pilot, flight attendant, and cargo handler you've ever exchanged words with. Nothing. You took temp jobs first in offices, clumsily faking your way through data entry, then retail work over the holidays, then at a warehouse where you loaded boxes of computer cables onto trucks for nine-hour shifts, but nothing came to a permanent income. There on the street you get a sick sensation in your stomach and suddenly feel like you might vomit, though you can't remember the last time you actually did.

Carter hails a cab and you slide in uneasily between Fisk and Winarski. Carter gets in the front. There is another man—his nametag says *McInheney*—who stands on the curb. "Let's get two," he says.

"Take us to where the river is green," Carter says to the driver. Winarski shuts the door and McIlheney yells, "Hey!" with his arms thrown up.

"Fuck him," Carter says. "You see him kissing up to Mancinelli? Company man."

The cab pulls over at a bridge. You all pile out and make your way through the throng left over from the parade to where you can peer down to the water. It is green but only its usual murky shade.

"It's pretty neat," Fisk says cautiously.

"We missed it," Winarski groans at him. He exhales loudly through his nose, and you get the impression that only some kind of reluctant decorum is preventing him from adding to the sentiment.

"Damn it," Carter says, leading the group on over the bridge.

You glance up at the planes flying overhead. DC-10. Airbus 330. Triple-7. You can tell them by their sound, these beautiful machines.

Across the bridge, cordoned off in a park running along the river, a group of a hundred or so protesters chant over the din of the crowd and traffic. Everyone is bundled in parkas and scarves against the cold. Behind them, the park is dotted with tents, cheap triangular ones that remind you of the ones you used to use when you were a Boy Scout. A tent city. The protesters grasp and shake tall signs with their gloved hands. You squint to read them. Most are versions of slogans you've heard over the last year: *We are the 99%. Stop the War on Workers. The People Are Too Big To Fail.* Some are cleverer: *Trickle Threat. Yes We Camp.* Your eyes focus longer on *I Lost a Job and Found an Occupation.* Revelers knock into you as you slow to witness the movement.

"Will you look at this shit?" Carter says, waving a disgusted hand toward the group. He calls out, "Pick your moments, people. It's a friggin' holiday."

"I think they know that," you say and point at one woman's sign that reads, *Drive the Real Snakes Out.*

"There's a time and a place," Carter said decisively. "They can get out and talk all the nonsense they want, but can we have a second's peace to have a good time?"

"There," Winarski says, pointing at a tavern just up the street. You get there and find a pile of protest signs leaning against the wall next to the door. The one on top says *What Would Daniel O'Connell Do*? Inside, you shimmy through the crowd. Fisk orders a round of car bombs, and you watch as the others drop their shots into black half-pints and drink it all down, then do the same.

"You keep it close to the vest, eh?" Fisk says, wiping his mouth with the back of his hand.

"What do you want to know, man?" you say, the warmth of the bar combining with the alcohol in your stomach to make you feel amenable to almost any discussion. "I'm an open book. I don't even own a vest."

"What's your line?" Carter asks.

"Pilot," you say.

The group looks at one another.

"Bullshit," Winarski says.

"Are you being straight with us?" Fisk says, a smile creeping into his lips. You've seen this look before. He wants you to be a pilot. You are exotic and manly.

"I wouldn't not be straight with you. I am a licensed and professional commercial pilot."

Carter challenges: "Which outfit?"

"I've flown for a few," you say. "But currently I am a freelance operator. I am ready to take you and your guests to any destination you desire. All I need is fuel money and a plane."

Winarski says "Bullshit" again, and Carter says, "Let's see some proof." You take out your wallet and show them your FAA license.

"So you can go see your wife," Fisk says, smiling. "What are you complaining about?"

"Who's complaining?" you say.

"Where's his wife?" Winarski says.

"Where's she again?" Fisk asks.

You eye a clock behind the bar—a real clock this time—and say, "Memphis."

Fisk scrunches up his face. "Was that it?"

"What happened?" Carter asks. "Why aren't you flying now?"

You shrug. "No jobs."

Winarski mutters, "Fucking Arabs."

The group standing next to you is clearly a part of the protest just up the street. Probably those are their signs leaning outside. They are a collection of three women and three men, all of them in their early twenties, one of them wearing a PETA T-shirt, another in one that reads *Obama*, with a clover in place of the O. All of them look to you like nice, conscientious college students. Good for them, you think. You didn't go to college, heading instead to the Navy for two years and then straight through flight training. You've regretted that decision more than a few times, not going to regular school, and you wonder for a moment if there might be a way to defect to this other party, to leave Carter and Fisk and Winarski behind and join up with these smiling kids.

"You Irish at all?" Fisk asks you.

"Everybody's Irish today," you declare loudly, and the group of kids, along with Fisk and Carter, raise their glasses and cheer your words. It feels possible that these two groups might merge, that you are all the same in good, drunken, basic ways.

More people file into the bar. A group of four black men, two of them with plastic green derby hats atop their heads, take a table by the window. Winarski taps you on the arm slowly, says, "They Irish today?"

His grin tells you that this is a challenge, a test to see how you will react. You shrug weakly.

"Hey," he says to you, that grin expanding into a smirk. "Leprecoons."

"What'd you say?" one of the college girl's voice issues from behind Winarski. She is small and pale and freckled.

"What?" Winarski says, irritated, turning his head halfway.

"I heard what you just said."

"Congratulations. Now mind your own business," Winarski says.

You try to take a step back, to disassociate yourself from Winarski, but only step on someone's foot and hear, "Hey, watch it."

"Fucking racist," the girl says.

"Why don't you go occupy somewhere else?" Winarski says, turning fully to her and her friends. "Before I get annoyed."

Two of the men in her group, both small and wiry, squeeze between the girl and Winarski, doing their best to make themselves appear bigger than they are. It is of little use. Winarski scowls down at them. Carter and Fisk notice what is happening and flank either side of you.

"This is a grown-up holiday, children," Winarski says. "Run along."

"Hey, I'm Irish," the girl says from behind her friends.

"He says everyone's Irish today," Winarski says, hitching a thumb at you, a note of amusement in his voice.

"Well, fuck him, too," the girl says. These words hurt more than you can understand. No, you want to say, I'm with you. I'm one of you. But of course you aren't. You don't even understand their movement completely. You look at them and then at Winarski and you can see the confusion.

"You got a lip, little girl," Winarski says.

"No, you know what," one of the little guys says, directing his words at not only Winarski, but at you, too. "Go on, enjoy it. This is the end for you all. The whole world is on to your

game. Your racist, capitalist patriarchy is finished, gentlemen."
He raises his beer. "One last party before extinction.
Good riddance."

Winarski leans toward the kid. His face is terrifying, red
and taut, his mouth pulled into a snarl. Carter puts a hand on
his shoulder, says, "Easy. Shit."

—

Out in the cold, darkening air of the late-afternoon, Winarski
says, "Little faggot."

And so here is the situation: you are engaged with a man
who has clearly demonstrated angry and possibly violent
tendencies. It would be easy enough to drop back from the
group, say, "You know, I think I'm going to head home." But
just as that scenario develops in your mind, you remember
that you have no home. "Don't worry about me," you said
to Sally last night before slipping into sleep for the last time
in your bedroom, already stripped of all furniture save the
mattress. "Really," you said. "You've got the girls. That's
enough for you to handle. I'll be fine." You even managed to
conjure a smile, though you had no plan. And you still don't.

Your decision is made when Fisk comes up beside
you and says, "He's not that bad, really. This has just been a
tough week."

You walk with them in silence into another bar.

"I'll tell you what the problem was yesterday," Carter says.
The four of you crowd around a tiny round table, little bigger
than a dinner plate. The mood of the day has shifted. Your
three companions each display their own version of a scowl.

"We got dick for sales," Winarski answers.

"We get no support," Carter counters. "What's the use of
any of those sons of bitches if they don't support us? You know
what you got with Mancinelli and the rest? You got the rich

ones like them and then you got everybody else. Where are we? Down in the soup with the homeless and the crackheads. No difference as far as they're concerned. Hell if they care about the men who get up every morning and go to work. This is a city here." He gestures out the window to the dusk-covered street. "You know, people work here. Cincy is a city. But these guys—." He takes a swig of beer. "You get the irony? Them all set up in their corner offices. But they can't *do*. You see? When it comes to sales, these fuckers need to bring us into their town. And still they manage to fuck us."

The minutes and hours begin passing more quickly as the sun slides away. The temperature crashes, but it has little effect as you all kick and stumble to another establishment, and then another.

In a sports bar, Fisk hands the group a round of Heinekens. "That fucking Mancinelli," Carter says over the music and the din of the bar, pointing his green bottle at Winarski and then Fisk. "He's the one that trips us up. He's the one setting the parameters and giving us up to these fuckers like yesterday." He guzzles at his beer. "Fucking Mancinelli," he says. "What's that neighborhood where he lives? I've got his address somewhere." Carter takes out his Blackberry and begins tapping at its keys. "We should get him where he lives."

"Get him?" Fisk says.

"Yeah, we should—."

"Absolutely," Winarski growls.

"We should go find his house," Carter continues. "Get some answers. He doesn't know what we do."

"We should go tell him?" Fisk asks.

"You know how much this week cost me in commission?" Carter says.

"Same as the rest of us," Winarski says.

Carter furrows his brow, says, "Yeah, well, close enough. Don't worry about it." Then his eyes go to the door of the bar, across the heads of the people around them. "With my kids in school," he says. "Fuckers toying with my family like it's some kind of game."

You think of mornings, walking Maeve and Franny to school, their backpacks sliding off their tiny shoulders, the way they do little jumps to hitch them back up. These are the best moments of your life, these mornings with your daughters. You do not know these men, nor their families. You don't even know what happened to them on this business trip that has them so upset. You don't want to know. Details will only muddy the perfect simplicity of their discontent. Something happened, or didn't happen, that has put their families in jeopardy. That's all you need.

"Let's go get the fucker," you say.

—

"I need an address," the cabbie says.

In the passenger seat, Carter one-eyes his Blackberry. "I'm getting it, I told you," he says. "It isn't like I'm withholding the goddamn information."

Back at the bar, struggling to think of where Mancinelli lives, the men told you to start naming neighborhoods. When you got to Lincoln Square, Carter stopped you, said, "That's it. Does that sound right?"

You shrugged.

Winarski demanded, "Is that a place a rich piece of shit is going to live?"

"I think the mayor lives there," you said.

"That's it," Carter said.

Now, in the cab, Carter tells the driver, "Lincoln *Square*. There's gotta be a corner. Probably four. Pick one and drop us there."

The cabbie sighs and pulls over at Lawrence and Western. Carter pays and glowers while the guy writes up a receipt.

The phone in your pocket buzzes. Once. Twice. It continues like Morse code. You know it's Sally, yet you can't bring yourself to answer. Her voice would change everything, bring you back to the world. You have no use for the world right now. Only the mission.

You want to get to this Mancinelli's house, to watch Carter and his men confront the guy, demand something of him, some explanation, compensation. An apology for whatever it was he'd done. The man needs to hear about Carter's kids, Fisk's and Winarski's families. What are *they* supposed to do while he, Mancinelli, the fucker, is enjoying the comfortable fruits of their labor. You want justice, even if it isn't your own justice. You want to see somebody squirm and then admit that he's been unfair, that there is a reason for everything that's happening and that this is what he's going to do to fix it all.

"I think I remember it being a name—the street—like Morris," Carter says, still tapping at his device as they walk past the shops and restaurants of the neighborhood. "Or Marvin."

"You're thinking of Monopoly," Fisk says. "Marvin Gardens."

"Morrison?" Carter says, ignoring Fisk. "I'm seeing it typed out." He squints into the distance. "Maxwell?"

In your pocket, the phone gives a quick double buzz. Voicemail.

"What are we going to do when we get there?" you ask.

"Just a little conversation," Carter says. "Just want to have a little conversation is all."

"What time is it?" Fisk asks, whiny. You want to tell Fisk to shut the fuck up with his questions. What does time matter?

"11:15," Winarski tells him, and you can't help but calculate the hours since the blue morning, estimate distances, conjure a road atlas in your head. What would be after Memphis? You should know this. Jackson?

Where are your wife and daughters? Jackson, Mississippi.

"What about here?" you say, pointing to a street sign. "Wilson."

"That's not an 'M'," Fisk says.

"He didn't say it was an 'M'," you snap. "He said it was a name."

You take them into the dark of this street, canopied by thick, bare branches. Cars line the curbs. Tall, narrow stone houses loom on either side. Your head is filled with liquid and your limbs feel like they could bend any which way, like some rubber doll. You are drunker than you've ever been.

"Mancinelli!" Carter hollers into the canyon. "Come out here, you son of a bitch!"

"Come on!" you yell. "Come face your maker. Or makers, or whatever."

"Good one," Winarski says.

"Get on out here, you fucker!" Carter yells.

"Mancinelli!" you scream. It feels fantastic, like throwing off an anchor, like shedding weight.

"I don't know," Fisk says, almost to himself.

"You don't know what?" you demand.

"Fucking guy," Winarski says, putting a big paw on your shoulder. "No skin in the game and still a mean bastard." He yells, "Mancinelli, you fuck!"

"Shut *up*!" a voice counters from one of the hundreds of windows.

Winarski stops and slowly scans the buildings, like he's spotting a sniper. Then his voice booms with terrifying ferocity: "What piece of shit just said that?"

No response. A light in one window goes off, and he eyes that glass for a good long time before Fisk says, "You don't think that was him, do you?"

You continue another few blocks, taking turns at random. You know you're weaving, your feet crossing over one another every few steps, but it feels more like a dance than any kind of problem.

Carter and Winarski drop back, continuing to yell out for their boss every few seconds, and Fisk comes to your side. "There's this thing our company has," he says to you. "Sort of a newsletter? And every month it has a section called 'Arrivals and Departures,' and it lists everyone who left the company and everyone who's been hired. The departures list is always longer. A lot of salesmen on there. Guys we worked with for ten years. Guys who were there way before I came on, before we were doing computers, back when the company did office equipment. They keep hiring more executives in New York and here. There's only a few little regional offices like ours left." He pauses and glances back at the others. "I don't know," he says. "There's something going on. Something about manners, maybe? I wonder if it's just something like that. Like, how nobody has any manners anymore?"

"*Manners*?" you say incredulously. You find yourself disgusted with this man.

"I don't know," he says apologetically.

You emerge from the shady residential streets onto a major thoroughfare that you cannot name. Carter spots a bar and leads the gang across the four lanes with a finger pointed the whole way to the other side, like a man at bat calling a homer. The bar is empty, the local news playing on a TV in the corner. Booze boxes line the back wall. Carter manages to get a round of Buds from the sleepy bartender and mumbles to Fisk and Winarski, "You fuckers better be keeping your receipts." In a plastic booth, you slurp and spill your beer, then turn to the bartender and say, "You know a guy named Mancinelli?" He ignores you, keeps on looking at the TV.

After another round, Carter declares loudly, "This must be the goddamn worst bar in all of Chicago."

The bartender breaks his silence, shouts, "Well, get the fuck out then, motherfuckers!"

Back in the cold, Winarski takes off his coat and swings it like a propeller blade. The street is abandoned. When Carter and Fisk duck into an alley to piss, you say to Winarski, "Think we're going to find him?"

"Mancinelli?" he says. "No. I don't."

"You need to keep hope, man," you say. "Keep hope alive."

"That asshole lives miles from here."

"You know his address?" A wave of excitement washes through you.

"Shit, I been to his place. Last year on another sales trip. Big penthouse type deal by the water."

"Why didn't you say anything?" you say.

Winarski puts his coat back on and sucks at his teeth. "I got kids. Think I'm going to lose my job just so I can tell this guy to go fuck himself?"

So then you understand: you were never meant to find him. It has all been pretend. You're just drunk and wandering toward nothing, puffing your chest out into the wind.

You've never hit anybody before and so it's actually more of a push, your loose fist onto Winarski's cheek. Surprisingly, it knocks him off balance enough that he hits the ground. But he gets back up and with disorienting swiftness he takes hold of your coat and lays a punch into your jaw. Your legs collapse beneath you.

The other two get back and Fisk says, "Jesus."

Carter comes in and presses Winarski back a few steps.

"Okay," he says. "Enough. Christ."

"What's with this fucker?" Winarski says. "Who is this guy anyway?"

"He's nobody," Carter says, still standing between you and the man who just laid you out.

"Leeching off us all day," Winarski says. "Sucking up our per diem."

"It's fine," Carter says. "It's over. Let's go."

"Who the fuck is this guy?" Winarski says to Fisk.

"I don't know," Fisk says.

"Let's go," Carter says again.

"We're going?" Fisk says.

"Cab, hotel," Carter declares. He pushes Winarski gently.

"Fly away now," Winarski says to you.

Fisk looks down at you, his soft face twisted into an apologetic question, and then follows the others. They are halfway down the block before Winarski turns and yells, "You ain't a fucking pilot!" These words seem to rip something from you, hurt you more than Winarski's fist. An ache grips your gut. You feel for your wallet in your pocket, your FAA license.

Once they have left, the city is utterly empty. Cars speed past, but you can detect no people behind their light-reflecting window glass. You have never been so completely alone. You step into the alley and piss. That ache in your stomach returns and you vomit next to a dumpster. When the sickness passes, you lean into the wall and listen to the voicemail on your phone.

It's me. We're stopping. I can't keep my eyes open. We're, I don't know, somewhere in Mississippi, getting close to Jackson, I guess. The girls are asleep. It's been a long day. We've had to stop every two hours. They're fine, but they know something's up. They're not stupid. If you get this in the next half hour or so, call, but I need to sleep. I hope you're in a motel or something.

We should be at my folks' by mid-afternoon, so we can talk then. Don't forget you need to call the guy at the storage unit about that discount in the paper. They need to honor that. Okay.

You listen to it again. The sound of Sally's voice echoes through your head. You can see Maeve and Franny asleep on a shared hotel bed, each spread out, their arms crossing one another's in the middle of the expansive mattress. Sally would have insisted on removing the hotel blankets and replacing them with the pink and purple ones she set in the backseat this morning. She never liked hotels, Sally. But she would be asleep by now herself, exhausted from the hours of driving and the long months of worry and struggle and uncertainty. You begin walking down this unknown street, stumbling forward into the cold, blustering air, past the bar you just left, past apartment buildings and warehouses and offices, past graffiti you can make no sense of, and past dim, buzzing streetlamps. You carefully orient yourself at the next intersection and head not towards your car, your neighborhood, but the opposite way, towards downtown, stepping deliberately, trying not to look like a lumbering nut, a drunk, some homeless fool.

—

The protesters' encampment is quiet. Yellow police barricades have been placed to define the space. Pairs of cops stand at each corner of the park, and they watch as you enter. Two dozen tents spike up from the ground. There are no campfires, no cooking stoves. Women and men huddle in groups of three or four, speaking quietly to one another. Others read by flashlight or whisper into cell phones. You pass by a couple, the girl leaning back against the boy, both of them covered with an unfurled sleeping bag. They look up at you and smile.

It is not what you expected. No one beats drums. No one leads chants. It is so quiet. Their signs stand propped up against lampposts. *Born Again American, We Are the Righteous Future.* A torn piece of cardboard on the grass reads, *A Better World is Possible.*

From the park you can see the bar where you were earlier in the day, where the Irish girl and her friends foolishly stood up to Winarski. The beer neons still shine, and the windows are hazy with the breath of the people inside. You wonder if you might find her. You'd like to explain who you are. But your mind cannot retrieve the details of her face. She could be any of these girls. And anyway, what would you tell her? Who are you? A grounded pilot. A man without a home. A father without children.

Tomorrow you will follow the path your wife and daughters set today. Of this you are sure, resolute, the decision having been formed not in any instant, but through the long hours since they left this morning. You will go to Texas and see about making a life there. But for now you simply watch the Chicago River lap against the embankment, the reflected city tousled in its current. The air sweeps past, filling your ears with its gusting roar, drowning out all else, and you close your eyes, imagining that your wife and daughters are here, striding to you across the grass, between the tents, all of them excited, having missed you during their time away. They reach you, and Sally's lips touch yours and she laughs, asks if you've been drinking. Maeve and Franny's fragile hands grab at your legs. The wind comes on stronger now, colder, and you lean down, wrap your arms around their small bodies, and rise against gravity to lift them up.

Traveling Light

Edie

Tucker comes in through the kitchen dragging the mingling smells of sweat and lumber. Sawdust sticks to his forehead and stubble and thin ponytail, and he says to Edie, who is seated on her high stool at the registration counter, "Broke a damn bit here." He holds up two thin shafts of metal, forming a V off the tips of his fingers. Says, "Second goddamn one since I started this thing." Tucker is building a small deck off the back of the hostel, a little sitting area for guests to use when the weather's nice, seldom as that is in Houston. "Back in a while," he says.

"Okay," she says casually, too casually, without looking up. He clomps toward the front door, but not before he gives her a look, the maudlin, quixotic glance of sexual victimhood that he's been shooting her way at increasing intervals ever since she told him that she didn't think they should sleep together anymore. They've been together only twice and when Edie thinks about these times she feels a cringe of guilt, as if she has used him in some or all of the ways that this look of his is meant to imply. As if he wanted a long-term situation any more than she did. As if her rejection of him has anything to do with his broken drill bit, easy symbolism aside.

Edie feels the hot air on her face when the door opens. Margot comes in. She's been sweeping at the dust and pine needles that gather on the concrete floor each day and night. Tucker says to her, "Earning your keep as always, huh?"

Margot smiles and says, "Yes."

Tucker hitches a thumb toward Margot. "I'm starting to think this one's got it figured out."

"Easy," Edie warns.

"Luckiest thing ever happened to this woman was running into you."

Edie says, "Shut the thing, will you." Tucker groans at the both of them and leaves.

Despite the heat, and as always, Margot is dressed in an ankle-length black skirt and a black cotton sweater that has faded to a singed charcoal. Her hair is black and gray and tied back. She comes to the desk and hands Edie a pile of mail, nods at Edie's "Thank you," and then shuffles to the parlor and takes up a feather duster, starts going over the side tables and door jambs and window ledges. The first floor has three rooms: a front parlor; a dining area, which doubles as a one-station, by-the-minute computer café; and a well-organized kitchen. Upstairs there are two dormitory style rooms, men's and women's, and one private room with a double bed that rents for ten dollars more per night.

Margot passes the duster across the rough wood of the mantle in the parlor and then starts in on the coffee table, moving aside the many issues of *Travel* and *National Geographic*, copies of *Desolation Angels* and *Slaughterhouse 5* and *Sophie's World* left there by various passers-through.

"You need to leave some of that for the boarders, sweetie," Edie says. It's hostel policy that guests help out with the cleaning the morning after their stay. She rests her chin on her hands. "Every day I have people asking what they can do and every day I look around and you've already done it."

"I don't mind," Margot says in her slow lilt.

Margot holds up a hardcover Africa photo book, admires it for a moment, and then cleans it. She puts the book down and goes to the dining room.

Edie looks through the mail and is surprised to find an envelope addressed to *Margot Rorsch c/o Travelers Hostel*. She has never, in her two months of residence, received mail here.

"Something for you," she calls.

Margot ambles slowly to the desk and gazes upon the envelope as if it was addressed in some foreign language, then takes it into the parlor. Edie can hear the shuffling of paper, then silence.

"Three is booked tonight," Edie calls.

Margot stays in room three, the private room, most nights. Budget-minded travelers usually opt for the dormitory, but Edie does not charge Margot for either. There have been few nights since Margot came to stay there that all the beds have been booked. On those nights, Margot simply disappears. Edie does not ask where she stays, but assumes the shelter downtown. That's where she had been staying before the two women met. Edie has never been there, but can imagine enough that she doesn't want details.

Edie grabs the bed assignment sheet and follows Margot as she climbs the stairs and hefts her green duffle into the hall. "Let me help you with that," Edie says. It is not heavy, but the sort of floppy, low-slung tote that begs to be dragged across the freshly swept floor. A poor child's sleep-over bag. The dormitory is empty. "Looks like you have your choice, with the exception of..." She checks the sheet. "One, four, and seven. Now, where we going?" Margot points to bed five and Edie slings the bag beneath it. Margot slumps onto the bed, the frame creaking under her. She is a large woman. Not obese, but certainly significantly bigger than Edie, who barely kisses the five-foot mark and who, at forty-four, remains as slight as she was at twenty.

"Tired?" Edie says.

"A little."

"Go on, take a nap," Edie says. Margot lays down on command and closes her eyes.

—

Edie and her husband, Mario, divorced two years ago. He left Lubbock for a job in Oklahoma and took his children, Edie's two stepsons, with him. His kids, so of course they would go with him. But it left Edie in the anguished position of having to say goodbye to the boys she'd half-raised for the past decade. Their mother had passed away, breast cancer, when the youngest was only three. Edie met Mario, a widower with two sons, a couple years later and fell in love with the boys, who were affectionate and silly and charming, as much or more than with the man. Then a decade later, her relationship with Mario deflated. He'd become something other that the man she'd met when she was thirty-three: a distant and dull person without purpose or social life or the need for either beyond his job, a person who, after the boys went to bed each night, fell wordlessly into the dank, polluted caverns of the Internet. She did not mourn her separation from him. They had become indifferent to one another, without enough passion between them to even spark a fire of animosity. Losing the boys, however, was agony.

She came to Houston and put her end of the cash from the sale of their house down on the hostel. She wanted to do something significant. Not as a replacement for the life she'd lost, but as a distraction. And she wanted to add to the value of a place. Edie herself had never traveled much—a few times to Phoenix as a child, once to Santa Fe to visit a girlfriend,

twice to Dallas for Cowboys games with Mario and the boys—
and had hardly heard of a hostel when the opportunity came
along. But she immediately liked the idea of hosting people
from around the world, of having these young ambassadors
from China and France and South America stay with her
for a night or two. She packed her clothes and dishes and
photographs. She shipped her few pieces of furniture in one
of those pod containers and then got into her Chevy (her own
pod container, she had thought at the time) and aimed herself
southeast.

For the first few months after the move to Houston, Edie
battled with Mario for contact with the boys. She called daily,
asking, then demanding, then all but begging to be able to
just talk to them. Mario contended, though, that it would only
confuse them, only stunt the transition to their new lives. So in
addition to half the house and a minimal alimony, the divorce
awarded Edie the stepparents' curse: a severing. A decade of
loving and nurturing nullified with a judge's signature due to
the lack of blood between them. But what of everything else?
What of the sweat as she walked them through the summer
streets of Lubbock? What of the tears seeped into the shoulder
of her shirt as she held them as they felt the ruining rush of
childhood embarrassment? What of the puke and piss and
shit wiped away? And the wounds: the scrapes cleaned, the
cuts bandaged. No blood? They've been amputated from her
and the thick crimson spills from her heart each day.

—

The hostel is impossibly quiet. Turns out Houston isn't the
international travel destination she thought it might be and
most days have been slow. Yes, Edie gets a few folks per week,
sometimes coming in from overseas, but most of the kids are
American, a lot of soon-to-be graduate students stopping in

town to check out Rice or U.H. She likes them just fine, but it gets lonely. Nights. It is in these moments that her mind invariably turns to sex. Thus the two encounters with Tucker, who she inherited as a handyman when she bought the place, along with a leaky roof and a fridge with bum coils.

She had been with five men before her husband and did not worry about missing out on numbers seven or eight or twelve. Her thirty-three-year-old self—consumed with the excitement of marriage and whatever vague conception of the American Dream that compact (even with someone as dull as Mario) brought to mind—was confident that these physical needs would shrink in the face of the more important matters of *building a life*. Now, though, this new self, this self-sufficient urban woman, this small-business owner whose enterprise was recently featured in the *Chronicle* in a series entitled "The New Faces of Houston," finds herself spending hours of each day fantasizing about what certain of her guests' skin might feel like. She replays episodes from her past, even the bumbling moment her virginity was lost in a basement on two couches pushed together front to front, the way they'd begun to spread apart and she, with James Ericson's weight on her, began to slip down, her back bare and suspended over empty space. She creates men in her mind, non-specific bodies and voices made more from what they aren't than what they are: anything but the cowboys and doughy, overgrown frat boys of Lubbock. More different still from her sluggish ex.

Of course, she knows that sex is only a substitute for something less definable, less visible. She desires communication, connection. She craves it like iron, like salt. To ask this of Tucker would be a joke. His anger toward the world which failed to live up to his early kind-bud and free-love expectations is a thick and constant cloud around his perceptions of others. Perhaps, Edie thinks, she is one more in a line of his disappointments: another woman that simply *doesn't get it*.

Edie wanders slowly through the rooms of her hostel, swiping a hand across the occasional surface as if to confirm the solidity of the tables and counters and chair backs. In the parlor, she finds Margot's letter sitting unsheathed on the coffee table, the envelope empty next to it.

She met Margot outside the public library downtown. In a further attempt to shed herself of the memory of her failed suburban experiment, Edie joined a group of young vegans who gathered twice a week with pots of lentil stew and crates of bananas donated by the Whole Foods and dished the food to stooped, bearded men who were, to Edie's happy surprise, generally talkative and cheerful despite their situation. There was only one other woman that night and it didn't occur to Edie at first that she could be there to be fed. The streets were one thing for all these men, but for a woman? Unthinkable. Margot lined up and slowly took a plastic plate, her eyes downcast.

Edie knows that even more than connection or conversation, she wants to be needed. The boys needed her. Perhaps Mario did too at one point, in his own inscrutable way. She feels that perhaps Margot does. This is, of course, why she asked the woman, a stranger to her that night at the library, to stay with her. What is a person, she wonders, if she is not essential to another, if there is not someone in the world for whom she is as crucial as breath?

Edie has never asked much about Margot's life; a woman's past was her own, as far as she was concerned, unless she wanted to reveal it. But there were times that it grated on her, the way Margot revealed so little. Edie would find herself chattering on about her life in Lubbock, about growing up there, driving streets abandoned save for the other teenagers like herself. "Real *Last Picture Show*-type stuff," she'd say, only to be met with the usual averted eyes, or perhaps—Edie hoped, anyway—a nearly imperceptible nod of understanding. Margot has heard about Edie's divorce and her move to Houston. She knows about Edie's fears in those first few weeks and months of this new life. She has once even seen Edie's tears upon mention of the boys. Edie shares.

She knows, of course, that there must be some pain in Margot's past, perhaps pain beyond what Edie can imagine, and she suspects that Margot is not fully functioning mentally (though she wonders what definitions of "functioning" she is using in this diagnosis). She likes Margot, she does. And she values having another woman around, if only to play unwitting interference now that Tucker is on the pity prowl. But their relationship is like a valve, letting the materials of friendship through one way, but not the other. Edie knows that Margot is originally from Illinois. This small bit of information was the result of the one direct question surprisingly answered. Most of the time she evades or mumbles or simply hunches her shoulders and shuffles away. It frustrates Edie, and it is this frustration that impels her to slowly unfold the correspondence from that morning.

> *Margot,*
>
> *I hope this letter reaches you. I've been waiting a long time to pin down an address where I might be able to reach you. I hired someone, a man who specializes in finding people. He got a record from a hospital in Flagstaff. I hope you are okay. Are you taking any medication? Is someone looking after you? I've tried to keep up with new diagnoses and treatments over the years, wondering if one of these new pills or regimens would be right for you. There are miracles happening in medicine, you know, treatments that turn people right around. In fact, I ran into Dr. Rose*

just the other day and he asked about you. I wish I had something to tell him.

Is this you, Margot? Do you remember me? I hope this is you, sister. I haven't felt this sort of hope in all these years. I want to tell you everything. I teach riding full time now. Maybe you're still riding. Maybe an old quarterhorse like Boo. I can't look at a bay without thinking of him and you. But mostly I want to tell you about Toby. He's thirteen now. He's been a wonderful child, Margot. His happiness is infectious. Before you brought him to me I'd never known joy of that sort. He's been the purpose of my life and I can't help but think that had you been here to witness him, to come to his Little League games and school plays, even if I had taken primary responsibility, you would have had that sense of completeness too. Through the years I've seen so much of you in him, which both thrills and terrifies me. He doesn't like to talk about you, but I know he wonders where you are. I see it in his face when your name comes up.

Write back to me, Margot. Or call or email. Please let me know that you are alright and safe. I love you.

Your brother,
Paul

Edie finds her hands shaking the papers audibly. She is unaccountably upset by what she has read. An email address and phone number follow the signature. The return address on the envelope says *Park Ridge, IL.* She goes to her computer and finds Park Ridge on a map, right next to Chicago. She wonders for a moment what that Midwestern city must be like, then remembers a book left at the hostel, a thin, beat-up old book of photography with a torn cover. She goes to the front parlor and eases the book out of its tight quarters on a shelf. *Shared Chicago*, it's called, and inside she finds street scenes, pictures of people. By the clothes they are wearing,

Edie figures the pictures must have been taken in the sixties or seventies, but the faces are no different from those she sees on the streets of Houston every day.

The letter is still in her hand. She wishes she had not read it. It isn't the simply disloyalty of the act, but now she finds herself in a quandary of responsibility. She hopes Margot will walk down those stairs and ask if she might use the phone long distance. Doubts it, though. The words linger in her mind: medication, treatments. And this Toby. The implication is clear enough. The story, though, is missing. Edie scratches the phone number onto her ledger, refolds the papers, and places it back on the coffee table, where she watches it from her spot at the registration counter.

—

Margot comes with Edie out back to check on the progress of the deck. It's night and the neighborhood is quiet. The frame is built and the lumber for the surface is stacked against the siding of the house. Edie is impressed at the speed with which Tucker is working. At this pace he'll be done in just a few days. Tucker joins them, packs a bowl and lights it, inhaling deeply, making the pipe whistle. He passes it to Edie who takes a smaller hit, the smoke clawing at her throat. In moments like these, when she is afforded a view of herself, she is amazed. Look at her here smoking marijuana like some mildly illicit second nature. She marvels at how her life has changed in the past year. What would Mario think if he saw her right now? She feels a deep relaxing, the pot taking effect, her soul sighing.

Margot motions toward the bowl in Tucker's hand, a silent request. "Well, sure," Tucker says. "Not like it cost me the money I work for."

"No?" Margot says.

Tucker hands her the pipe and says, "Bright bulb, huh. Quick wits."

"Oh, shut up," Edie says lightly. But then there's that look again, hurt and horny at once. Lobbying for a pity fuck. Not going to happen, my friend.

The pipe goes around again and Tucker says he's got to go, says something about some people having to get up in the morning, and its clearly meant as a swing at Margot. She doesn't show any sign that the punch landed. Anyway, Tucker knows that Margot is up every day before he arrives.

"Can I ask you something?" Edie says to Margot, now they are alone, sitting in a couple of beat up old camp chairs. "Who is Toby?"

"Toby?"

"I read your letter," Edie says. "I'm sorry. I shouldn't have, but I was curious. I feel like I don't know much about you."

"Toby," she says, as if trying to find the right answer. "I think he's my nephew." She looks up at the washed out sky. "Yes, he's my brother's boy."

"Oh," Edie says. "I thought maybe he was—" she stops. "Because of what it said I thought perhaps the relationship was different."

Margot's eyes dart over at Edie twice and Edie is struck by how alert they seem. Has she been misreading this woman? Has she been getting fooled?

"I don't know anyone named Toby," Margot says.

Edie waits a moment, her eyes still on Margot. "No?" she says.

"No. I think that letter was not for me. Now that I think about it."

"You had horses growing up?" Edie asks, ignoring the denial. "A horse named Boo?"

Margot changes positions in her chair, shifting to her hip as if about to roll off the side.

"I'd like to help if I can," Edie says. "I know how much I miss my boys. I mean, I can imagine—"

"I think I'd like to go to bed," Margot says. "I'm going to go to bed in the dormitory."

—

It is the next evening before Edie picks up the phone and dials the number for Margot's brother in Illinois. She spends the hours between being nagged by the conscience of a betrayer, not only because she is going to insinuate herself, unasked, in the life of another woman—a *friend*, she has decided—but because that night and periodically through the next day she finds herself thinking about this brother, Paul: what he'll sound like on the phone when she calls, what words he will use to express his happy relief and his gratitude. She gives the Paul of her mind no particularly distinguishing feature, no extraordinary height or shoulder width, no gray, romance-novel eyes. Beyond an imagined conversation from thousands of miles away, he remains to her only a notion, but a notion that she feels she might understand on some level, and that might understand her. She knows that she may never meet him, and this is why it takes as long as it does for her to make the call. She wants to hold onto the possible for as long as she reasonably can. She must call, but perhaps tomorrow, perhaps later, in just an hour, in ten minutes, in just, just...

Her fingers shake as boarders descend the stairs and leave the hostel, as the open door breathes humid evening air across her face, as she dials the phone and feels the full tonnage of her loneliness.

Paul

The porch of this ramshackle stone building is cracked. He wonders if it is foundational. There are two birds on a table outside the door, thin black things with yellow eyes. They look to Paul like crows gone bad, like ravens tweaked out on crystal meth. They look at him with their beaks spread open, as if panting in the oppressive heat. Watching them, Paul suddenly panics at not having prepared more. He is a blank, and feels stupid to have thought that the right words would simply conjure themselves. He is filled with an awful fusion of excitement and dread. What if she has left? No, this Edie woman surely would have called. What if she does not want to see him? She was the one to leave, after all; she has been the one to not return. What if her mind is too far gone to recognize him? Worse, what if he sees her and does not feel the great swelling of love and sibling allegiance that he has imagined so many times?

He pushes the heavy door and meets eyes with a small, elfin woman with short hair sitting behind a counter. Still in the doorway, he says, "I'm looking for Edie." He cannot yet say that he is here for Margot. Baby steps.

"Paul?" the woman says.

He closes the door behind him, straightens his sport coat, under which he is slicked with sweat. He nods and takes in the place. Stairs lead to a shadowy second floor. A front room appears to be some sort of quasi-Victorian parlor. The woman scoots off her stool and walks to him on light feet. She is even smaller than he had originally realized: tiny, a little sparrow of a woman. At six-foot-two, Paul feels strangely apologetic for his height.

"She's upstairs," Edie says. Her voice is quiet. He told her a bit about their history over the phone, not much, just a few details she couldn't have gleaned from the letter she'd read.

"Should I go get her?" Edie asks.

Paul exhales and nods, says, "Please." Then, quickly, "No. Can I have a glass of water?" He reasons that his throat is, in fact, dry, and isn't water just the trick for that. If it delays the impending moment a bit, gives him a few seconds more to steady himself, well. Edie nods and goes softly into what Paul figures is the kitchen. He steps into the parlor, away from the view of the second floor landing, ashamed of himself for hiding from the sister he's spent all this time searching for now that she is, what, fifty feet from him? Less?

Paul has not seen Margot in more than ten years, since, in the midst of a drug-enhanced psychological and emotional tailspin, she brought Toby to him, demanding that he take the boy into his home. It was not a surprise. Margot had always been troubled. As a teen she disappeared twice; the first time she was gone for a week, finally discovered sleeping in the basement of an Episcopal church off of Belmont Avenue in the city. The other incident lasted nearly two weeks, ending when a man from a small town called Sycamore fifty miles west of Park Ridge phoned and said he found her in his pasture, sitting in the dirt among the horses. She was hospitalized after the second disappearance and diagnosed with what the doctors called "mild schizophrenia," though Paul has always contended that this was akin to referring to a "slight amputation," the qualifier being a damn sight short of consolation. She was put on a series of treatments, from group talk therapy to heavy doses of Thorozine, and spent the next years of her life in states of zombified disconnection. It wasn't until she began work with Dr. Rose in her mid-twenties that she was able to live with anything like self-sufficiency, working periodically and moving into a shabby studio apartment in the Logan Square neighborhood.

Paul only met Toby's father once. Dale Dumont was a sullen and gaunt man with sinewy muscles beneath the brown-tanned skin of his arms, which were then covered in long and dark hairs. His eyes were ice-blue and his face pock-marked. Margot brought him to Paul's apartment after it was known that she was pregnant. Paul sat and listened while Margot spoke excitedly about the life they would provide for the child: the house ("Maybe somewhere around here, huh Dale?"), the top-notch schools, the love. Paul remained silent through these rants, knowing that to question her would only stack another brick in the wall that her brain chemistry had masoned between them so many years before.

Edie comes back with a glass of water. She is an attractive woman. He puts her in her early-forties, maybe just a little younger than himself.

"You run this place yourself?" Paul asks and immediately feels like a creep, like he's casing the joint. Or her.

"I get help. A man named Tucker. Handyman. And Margot. She helps out a lot, actually, tidying up and such."

Paul notices that the place is clean, despite the aged furniture and worn hardwoods.

"You're from Houston?" he asks.

"Lubbock," she says. "Past life."

"Married?" he says.

"Divorced," she says, then with a sad shrug, "the old story."

Paul himself never married. He supposes, when he has occasion to consider it, that he'd planned on a wife, inasmuch as any young man holds the vague notion in his mind. But when Toby came to him—Paul was thirty-five at the time—all plans were suddenly adjusted, if not scrapped altogether. He's dated women, sure, but at the end of these nights (or in the mornings, if things went in that happy direction and Toby was at a sleepover), he never felt the need for more permanent attachment. He has his work and he has Toby, and this has always seemed enough for him. There have been moments and periods of loneliness, of course. But he has heard married friends grouse about this same thing, so perhaps it isn't a matter of marital status. Perhaps it is simply a part of the human experience.

Edie tilts her head to the side. "Should I go get her?" She comes to where he stands and, as if they have known each other for years, puts a hand on his shoulder, says, "It's okay." She shrugs. "Your sister." As in, *Time doesn't change that.*

Edie ascends the stairs and disappears into the relative dark of a hallway. Not twenty seconds later she is back on the landing. Behind her is another woman, slumped and bosomy, black clad despite the ungodly heat, and in this woman's wide, chapped face, Paul sees his sister.

—

He stares at that face from across the small dining table. Her eyes remain downcast like he'd seen them when their parents or the police brought her home after one of her teenage sojourns. She has not said a word.

"I can tell you things," Paul says. "If you don't feel like talking, I can talk. I can tell you about home. You wouldn't recognize Park Ridge, the way it's been built up. I've got a place now out west of there, a stable where I teach. Can you believe that? After all the hours I spent as a kid complaining about being out at the barn. A nice place. Already getting cold up there, though. Not like here." Excellent, he thinks. The weather. Genius. He waits for anything to register on her face, any twitch or blink to let him know that she was there. "I can tell you about Toby," he says. He had meant to delay this, didn't want to spook her, wanted to gain her trust, maybe even wait until she asked. "He's a great kid."

"No," Margot says, as if coughing up the word.

Paul silences himself. He knows the Edie woman is

nearby, at her front desk perch, and this is comforting to him. Margot lifts her head and looks around the room slowly, a perturbed look upon that face of hers. She is breathing heavily. "Have you been to Houston before?" she asks.

Paul shakes his head.

"I'll show you," she says.

Edie hands over her keys without question. "I should have rented something," Paul says to her.

"Go," she says easily, a hand on his back, pressing him to where Margot waits on the sidewalk.

"Am I driving?" Paul says, to which Margot only glances at him quizzically on her way to the passenger door. It is the most demonstrative expression she has made since Paul arrived. She directs him to U-turn and then take a right here, a left there. She leans into the window, away from Paul, watching the buildings and trees and cars slip behind them. She says, "That's one of the museums."

"Uh-huh," Paul says, catching glances of her in his periphery.

"The park," she says.

"Uh-huh."

"Medical Center there."

"Speaking of 'medical,' can we talk about how you're doing?" Margot sighs, shakes her head. Paul says, "I'm just concerned, you know?"

She directs them downtown. "The library," she says. "Stop there."

He curbs the car and they wander around the hulking concrete building, unspeaking amid determined business-types and elderly exercise walkers. He notices a few people looking at Margot, or perhaps he's imagining it. He watches her. She walks a few feet in front of him, her shoulders slumped, leading the way, leaving it up to her feet to play an ongoing game of catch-up.

Finally, Paul gestures to a bench, says, "Sit down here." Margot does as he tells her. Paul can feel his stomach roiling. "I want you to come home with me," he says. "I'll buy you a ticket and we can go back together. Get you some help. Do you hear what I'm saying? I worry that you can't take care of yourself. You can stay with us, even help out at the stable if you want."

People hurry by, a few glancing at the two of them sitting there, a mismatched pair engaged in a conversation too serious for this public arena.

"This is all happening for a reason. Don't you see? I get word where you are and that very same week I run into Dr. Rose. After all these years. At the grocery store, for Christ's sake. He's got a private practice now. I'll bet you could go back to him."

Dr. Rose was a nearly constant presence in Paul's parents' house, with dinnertime conversations often revolving around what he had said about this or that symptom. They looked to him to confirm what they'd been seeing, to translate Margot's behavior into something comprehendible. It was as if Dr. Rose, through all this time, took on a significance in their lives that no person could live up to: he was order amidst the chaos; he was hope when Paul and his parents could not muster any of their own.

Paul can see Margot tensing up. "Easy," he says. "These are all good things."

"What does the kid think?" Margot says.

"Toby? He's all for it," Paul lies without thinking. The fact is that Paul has no idea what he is doing. The boy was eating dinner in the bungalow-style house they'd been living in for the past seven years when Paul got the call from Edie. He remained in the kitchen after hanging up, trying to steady his breath, trying to figure out how to act as if the whole world hadn't just suddenly changed. That night he arranged for Toby to stay with a friend for the weekend.

"Think about it," Paul says now. "You could be back for Thanksgiving."

Margot stares toward their reflection in a shop window across the street. "Okay," she says. And like that, he has his sister back. Though he has imagined this moment a thousand times, he can't now remember how he figured he would feel. He is bringing her home, and yet, there is no jolt of elation or even satisfaction. In all those moments of fantasy when he saw this transpiring, he hadn't thought of the future or even the present, but only of the past, as if he were going to be able to snatch back the Margot of years ago, pull her into the present. He had not thought to account for whatever transpired in the decade-plus between, those mysterious thousands of days he will never know about.

They stand and walk silently around a corner. Margot brings them to what looks like an elaborate park with a man-made reflecting pond and a fountain under which children in bathing suits run and cry out high-pitched shrieks of laughter. For the first time, Margot looks at Paul with something like a smile. She walks toward the fountain and then looks at him again. Now she is smiling. Smiling like Margot, like Paul remembers, mischievously. A smile, he figures, doesn't change. He grins back at her and then realizes she's going under the water. He stops. Margot laughs. Parents watch, inch towards their children.

"Hey, don't go in there," he says. "Come on. Come on, let's go get something to eat or something."

Margot laughs again and in her black sweater and black skirt she looks like some sort of maniacal angel of death. "Don't go in there," Paul says. Children are clearing out of the fountain. People keep their eyes on her. She goes under the cascading water, lets it push her hair down against her face. Her clothes weigh down heavily on her corpulent body. "Come out of there, for Christ's sake," Paul snaps, but she makes no move away from the water. He gets near her, the water splashing his shoes and pantlegs. "Let's go now." He quickly grabs her hand.

"No!" she shrieks, a piercing banshee screech. Paul recoils.

"Hey, buddy," a man says from behind.

"It's okay," Paul says, eyes still locked with his sister's. He puts both hands up in a gesture of surrender. Her body relaxes a bit and she resumes breathing. Paul takes a few steps backwards and Margot follows out of the water.

At the car, she sits in the passenger seat with a squish. He feels exhausted. Not just tired, but emptied, hollowed. Paul turns the radio on—something to fill the air—but is clobbered by the ridiculous bombast of the *1812 Overture*. He switches it off immediately. He recalls reading somewhere that Tchaikovsky was a little crazy, that he went off vagabonding through Russia for some period of his life, and that people suspect he killed himself. Paul has a hard time, though, reconciling the story of this sad man with the cymbal crashes and brass blasts echoing through his head. He says nothing of this to Margot, of course.

—

When they get back to the hostel, Edie is in the midst of preparing dinner. "Are you wet?" she asks Margot, and tells her to go change into something dry. "Well," Edie says to Paul, "how was your adventure?"

"She's coming home," Paul says.

"That's wonderful," Edie says smiling. "You must be so happy."

"I am," he says because it is what he is supposed to say. "Tell me about yourself," he says.

She smiles and sighs and says, "Well..." Then she tells him that she has owned the hostel for two years, that she bought it after her marriage ended. She pauses, turning to stir the pot of stew bubbling in a slow cooker. "It isn't the life I imagined," she says, "but I doubt anyone ever gets that." She cranks pepper from a grinder and Paul watches the muscles of her forearms flex beneath her tan skin. "I have two stepsons who went to Oklahoma with my husband," she says. Her back is to Paul but he can see in the curve of her shoulders that this sentence has devastated her in some small way.

"Do you get to see them?"

She shakes her head almost imperceptibly. "They aren't mine," she says quietly.

Toby's image alights in Paul's mind. Paul would take the boy to the various stables where he taught in the early days, and Toby would prop himself up on the small bleacher seats lining the arena and watch Paul direct his students to adjust their bodies in all the tiny ways that communicate so much to the animals beneath them. "Heels down," Paul would call. "Shoulders back. Hands up, like your holding two mugs." Each day before untacking the school horse, Paul would ask Toby if he wanted to get on, and each day the boy would shake his head no. Then one day he shyly—and to Paul's surprise—agreed. And when he did he was a natural, his form perfect. He went into a trot and posted up and down in the saddle evenly with the rhythm of the horse's gait and Paul was struck with what he felt for the first time must have been the pride of a father.

Paul watches Edie's small frame and is overcome with the urge to touch her, to place a hand on the fabric of her dress between her shoulder blades. He feels an unexplainable familiarity with her, as if he's known her for so much longer than these few hours. "My boy isn't—" he begins.

The back door bangs open and shut and a man comes into the dining room, a man about Paul's age, paunchy and stubbled, with a ponytail hanging down his neck. "Done," the guy says. "Still has to be stained, but otherwise, done."

"Wonderful," Edie says. She breathes in deeply and takes a stack of bowls down from a shelf.

"Who's this?" the man says.

"This is Paul," Edie says. She introduces the man as Tucker.

"Handyman," Paul says. "Right?"

"Contractor."

"Paul is Margot's brother," Edie says and a little smile contorts Tucker's expression.

"No shit," he says. He snorts out a laugh and says, "Alright." Edie gives the guy a look. *Mind your manners.*

Tucker says to Edie impatiently, "Well, don't you want to see it?"

"Yes," Edie says. "Of course I do."

"Geez," Tucker says.

Paul follows them uninvited through the kitchen and out onto a deck, about twelve by twelve. The planks feel sturdy underfoot. Paul's never been much for building things, though he admires the ability. "Nice," he says.

"Yeah," Tucker says, as in, *Yeah no shit it's nice, guy. What can you build?*

"It's perfect," Edie says, "Really." And this Tucker seems relieved. "We'll break it in tonight," Edie says. "Special occasion. Margot is going to be leaving us. Heading back to Illinois with her brother here."

Tucker gets a smirk on his face like he knows something. "Are you staying with us?" Edie asks Paul.

"He should stay in three," Margot's voice declares from the doorway behind them. "If it isn't taken." She has changed into a different long black skirt and a navy blue sweater. A small difference, but a difference nonetheless. A bit of color. Paul hates himself a little for appreciating that she looks a bit less crazy.

That evening they all share a quiet dinner, and then retire to the new deck, where Edie has set up folding chairs. The sky is clear, but the city lights wash out the stars. Edie brings out a jug of white wine that quickly goes to sweating out in the humid air. Paul watches as Margot sips from her glass. He still hasn't gotten any information about her mental state, nothing beyond what he's been able to witness, at least, which has seemed to be in some middle ground between what he'd expected and what he'd feared.

Edie extends her legs out and crosses them at the ankles. Light glints off her shins. He then finds Tucker watching him. Paul doesn't always get along well with other men; it's been this way his whole life. He has frequently wondered if this was one of the reasons he went into the equestrian world, a place where women outnumber the men ten-to-one, or more.

Ten feet past Tucker, the biggest cockroach Paul has ever seen is latched onto the side of the garage. "Jesus," he says.

"Palmetto," Tucker says and chucks a pebble at the wall. It skitters away and disappears into the shadows. "Twenty years and I still hate those fucking things," Tucker says.

"Nothing worse than a grumpy hippie," Edie teases him.

"Don't give me that business," Tucker says, then turns to Paul. "What do you think of our fair city?"

"Seems fine."

Tucker holds Paul's gaze for a second, then says, "Fine, fine, fine." He takes a short pipe out of his pocket and packs it. He takes a hit, the pipe whistling, his nose illuminated by the orange embers. Paul wonders how many years it had been since he saw someone smoke pot. He lives in a different world. "That's it? *Fine*?"

"I've been here all of eight hours," he says in his defense.

"Shit, that's plenty of time to catch the vibe of a place. To get its aura, if you've got eyes to see it."

"Aura?" Paul says, more of a challenge than he intended.

"The *feel*," Tucker says. "What it's about." He holds the bowl out to Edie, who waves a hand and says, "No." Tucker offers Edie a sort of sad-sack look and Paul figures there is something between them. Paul understands that normally Edie would have taken the pipe. And he knows that he is the reason she didn't this time.

"I guess," Paul says, getting back to the aura business.

"You guess," Tucker says. "Let me guess a little something about you."

"How about you don't," Edie says.

"Two-car garage," Tucker says. "Half of it filled with shit you never use. Got a half-finished basement. Maybe that's where you keep your tools, all of them expensive and brand fucking new."

"This is not interesting," Edie says.

Tucker seems to be readying another attack on one of them when Margot reaches a hand out towards him. It's as if she is going to lay it on his arm, perhaps to diffuse the situation with a calming gesture, but instead she motions for the pipe in Tucker's hand. She nods her head, asking permission. Tucker hands the pipe over, a smug grin across his face. "Anything for you on your last night in town," he says.

Paul watches her light and inhale and he is filled with a rage he knows to be indefensible. But understanding has nothing to do with the bile rising within him. This petty gesture cuts so deeply into Paul's precarious sense of solidarity with his sister that the feelings he has been pushing back like tidal waters all afternoon now rush out undeniably into his consciousness. She abandoned her son, left him to be raised by his uncle, and lit out for God knows where, never writing or calling, never giving a shit about those who loved her, who worried themselves sick every day for all these years. He does not want this woman coming into his home. He does not want her influencing his boy. His *son*. It has been all he could do to counter whatever troubled biological imbalances she passed on to him; what might happen when those physiological traits are now paired with this bloated manifestation of mental derailment. No, it is not love that Paul feels towards Margot. It is anger.

Paul launches himself from his seat and through the back door, into the hostel. He is at the foot of the stairs, ready to ascend and shut himself in the relative solitude of his rented room and call for a cab to take him back to the airport.

"Paul," Edie says.

She looks at him with the sad-eyed gaze of a person who doesn't yet know him. He is overcome with exhaustion and frustration and sadness.

"I'm not a good person," he says.

"Who is?" she says.

A rush of silence overtakes the room. His heart lurches in his chest as they look upon one another, both utterly still. Then Edie steps forward, bridges the gap between them. She cranes her neck up toward him and he, as if their mouths are magnetic elements, leans into her kiss. He knows suddenly and certainly that someday soon he is going to ask this woman to marry him.

Margot

"Goddamnit," Tucker breathes, shaking his head slowly, like he's moving it through water. "That brother of yours," he says. "Pretty quick operator, boy."

It has been a long day and she sits deep in her chair. Her stomach is full from dinner. The pot and wine relax her body. It is all nearly enough for her to pretend that her brother did not find her, that he is not here now, that she did not agree to return to her hometown tomorrow. She recalls the moment, only hours ago, in the park: she does not blame him. How could either have known that his hand would burn, that the touch of skin on skin would set her arm aflame? It has been so long. The orderlies in Flagstaff, they burned her, as did the police in Portland. Who else? The man in Reno, the dark of the alley made even darker by the blinding lights of the casino. Her parents in the shadows of the barn aisle outside Boo's stall. These hands that grabbed and restrained and scorched like acid. When she screamed he let her go, her blood pumping fast through her body, rushing, rushing, as if her heart might explode. He raised his hands and she could see that they were pulsing with red heat. Everything shimmered and flashed in the high sun.

She takes another hit from Tucker's pipe and the smoke embraces her from the inside.

Margot has been in Houston for nearly five months now. Before that, Tucson. Before that, a stint in Vegas and prior to that, as well as she can remember, Denver. She knows the major cities of the West and Southwest and high plains, though the events and chronology of her stays are fuzzy. She knows San Francisco's Haight Street and Golden Gate Park and Denver's Five Points shelters. She knows Portland's little downtown and how to get a free coffee off the kids at Powell's. She knows to avoid Seattle's Pioneer Square at night and

L.A.'s shelters almost completely, at all costs. Her memories of these all places have been etched in ink, permanent. Her sense of direction is keen despite the general confusion that increasingly defines her waking mind. She knows these towns like one knows language: without thought or memory of genesis. One does not remember the time they learned the meaning of *road* or *sky* or *lips*, nor does Margot recall the first time she wandered through these American cities, finding food or bedding down. They are simply a part of her, spun into her DNA.

People, though, are a different story. The ones from her earlier life, they're safe. She knows her brother. She can, but doesn't if she can force it from her mind, recall the face of Toby when he was young. Those from the last decade, though, they slip away: names, then faces, then times shared. She can recall crowded dormitories and communal dinners, but the people within those images are fuzzy outlines at best. Return trips to San Diego or Salt Lake or Omaha, of which there have been many over the years, are exercises in pretend and cover-up; she might be greeted at this hostel or that food bank, and she must discern a smile of recognition from one of simple affability. She will attempt vague conversations in hopes of gaining a name or history to go on. She knows the look when she fails to convince, too: a closed-lip smile followed by a pitying aversion of eyes. The imprint of these interactions remain for a while, sometimes years, but the details of the faces across from her, and their words, bleach away from her memory.

She rarely has to stay at the shelter anymore, since befriending Edie, only those nights when all the beds are booked. She likes it here quite a bit: likes the quiet and she likes Edie, who has kindness in her veins, same as too many people have sorrow and hate. Margot would prefer to stay on for as long as she is welcome, but she has told Paul that she will go with him.

Overcome with thirst, Margot hoists herself laboriously from the chair and swims through the humid air into the cool of the hostel kitchen. She drinks a glass of water and then another. It floods her body, each cell momentarily washed clean. She hears the creaking of the stairs and, stepping toward the front of the building, finds Paul and Edie walking side-by-side to the second floor, their slow steps synchronized, then disappearing into the hallway. She hears the familiar clunk of the door to room three closing.

Margot considers the new opportunity before her. She waits a few moments more before following up the stairs, stepping close to the banister where the wood creaks less. She can detect sleeping bodies in the dark of the dormitory. As quietly as she can, Margot retrieves her duffel and eases the door shut. Downstairs, Tucker is leaning against Edie's registration desk. He drinks from a small bottle of whiskey. "Where you think you're going?" he says.

"Atlanta," she says without thinking.

He laughs. "What, you walking there?"

"Hitch," she says.

"Fuck, lady. You are some kind of nut." He sloshes more whiskey into his mouth. "Even I know you can't catch a ride here in the middle of town. Even I know that." He looks up at the second floor landing. "So, you're bailing on little brother?" Margot does not respond. She is starting to feel her whole body burn.

"Come on," Tucker says. "I'll take you a little outside of town, get you to somewhere you can catch a real ride."

—

The night cools down and Tucker puts his hand out the window, holding it flat against the rushing air, and says, "Goddamn if it doesn't feel like this shit is finally breaking." He drives east on 10, past the bright billboards and retail signs, and each time Margot thinks he's going to pull off, he doesn't. He keeps going past the light of the outlying suburbs. He's drinking from that bottle and talking to Margot more than he ever has before.

"Think she's paying me?" he says. "What she's giving me for that deck barely covers materials. Think I'm tacking on the cost of those two bits I broke in the process? A lot of contractors would, you know. Some shady motherfuckers out there. Not me. I'm doing this thing because I'm a good guy. Because I like her and I've been working on that place for longer than she's been around, that's for sure. I'd just hate to see some character take advantage of her." He offers Margot the bottle and she takes a shot, hands it back. "You know," he says, "I thought you were doing that for a while there, taking advantage of her. That's why maybe it seemed like I didn't like you sometimes. I can see that you aren't, though. You're alright people. Fucking loony as the day is long, no denying that, but alright people."

They pass sleepy Beaumont and glide across the Louisiana border. Somewhere west of Baton Rouge, Tucker says, "Fuck, I'm a little shitfaced." He tests his eyes, winking one, then the other. "Yeah, this isn't a good idea. I tell you what. I suggest that we pull into a place where we can get a room. I'm going to pass out for a few hours and you can stay or be on your way or whatever you like. How's that sound?"

She can't remember the exact last time she stayed in a motel. Somewhere in Tacoma maybe. Maybe Missoula. She thinks of the nights spent with Dale Dumont in various hovels around Chicago, before she told him the truth about Toby and he left, them sitting on the edge of sunken beds and saturating their minds with whatever they could afford. They could make some plans, the two of them, on those snowy nights. They would build things in their ecstatic conversations: houses and careers, families and meals, clean bodies and spirits. They caught each other's words like snippets of dreams suddenly recalled, and ran that tiny notion into an entirely new idea of what was to come.

Tucker drives on in silence for some time, his shoulders slumped forward, before he mutters, "Some kind of smooth goddamn operator."

—

She remembers her horse, Boo, into whose amber eyes she fell. She can still feel the dense flesh of his neck under her hands. She can smell the sweet mingling of hay and manure through the stable. She can feel the rumble of his great torso under her as they circled the arena. She remembers Park Ridge, the town where she grew up. She knows its layout, or at least what its layout was two decades ago. She can picture the grid of arterial roads, the tree-canopied side streets; she knows where the grocery stood, where the schools are, where the city dug out a public pool when she was a kid. She closes her eyes and sees the house of her childhood, the walk up to the mahogany red door. The light comes through the picture window with blinding brilliance. Just inside, there is a stairway with framed pictures rising on the wall. This is the first time in years she has let herself look back this far. To the left of the entryway is a dining room; to the right, a living room with an expensive sofa near which no one is allowed to eat or drink. She hears a voice, coming from the kitchen. "Margot?" the voice says. "Margot, are you home?"

And she remembers the night Toby was created: her great secret, the details of which she has never told another living soul. Winter outside and blue dusk had slunk through the blinds into Dr. Rose's office. Margot could smell the alcohol on his breath. "Can I have some?" she said. He poured her a short shot of vodka in a water glass, and a taller one for himself.

"This stays here," he said. He took his usual seat and she took hers. Once a week or more, depending on how well she was coping, she met him in this office, sat in this chair and talked to him, verbalizing her fears, describing her moments of confusion, sometimes arguing with him about what was real and what wasn't. She'd watched his face change, lengthen and soften, over those years. She noted when his wedding ring disappeared for a time, then returned. She knew him intimately through these observations and through the questions that he asked. What was he preoccupied with this week? Family? Sex? God? She found out how much you could know about someone by the questions they ask, far more than by any answers they might give. People reveal themselves through their questions.

"You need more help than I can give you," he said despondently.

"I'm getting better," she said.

He breathed audibly, closed his eyes, and said, "You aren't."

"Ask me questions," Margot said. "Ask me questions and I'll give you answers."

His hands did not burn her that evening, nor did his belly against hers, his tongue in her mouth. After all those years, it felt so natural to have him inside her. She can recall marveling at the way their bodies fit together. As he finished, he emitted a deep lowing growl, and his body ceased moving on top of hers. She knew she had done well, pleased him, but the next week when he was distant towards her, averting his eyes and cancelling a number of upcoming appointments, she felt the heat rising in her for the first time in years. He placed a hand on her back, directing her out of the office, and it was as if she'd been branded.

—

Each day, regardless of where she might be or what time of year it is, Margot wakes twenty minutes before dawn. A habit of necessity formed from the need to be clear of doorways and vestibules before the people of the world wake. This morning, though, perhaps for the first time in years, she sleeps until seven. The room is still the same bruise purple as it had been hours before, when she and Tucker arrived and he fell onto the other bed, snuffling whiskey snores into the pillow. That bed is still made but imprinted with the heavy squash of his body. She waits until the clock reads seven-fifteen, then gets up, uses the bathroom and showers, dresses, and pulls open the curtains, light filling every corner of the room. It was pitch dark when they pulled in and the world around this little motel could have been forest or desert for all they could detect. Now, opening the door and stepping out of the room, bag in hand, Margot sees that that it is farmland. Tucker's pick-up is gone. A truck stop sits squat across the parking lot. On the far side of the truck stop is a fence and then pasture. The air is cool, perhaps still in the forties, and a downy blanket of fog rests upon the land. Low-lying hills form a wave on the horizon and live oaks slung with moss hunker in clusters. The smell of fuel permeates the air, but the wind brings along a familiar whiff of alfalfa.

She hears semis blowing past on the highway. A few pull off to gas up. Sitting on the hard angle of a parking block, her bag clutched to the chest, Margot watches as each driver descends from his cab, hopping or stumbling with stiffness. She waits for the right one, the safe and kind one that will take her on. After four or five, she sees him. He is of medium height and build (too heavy might indicate a drunk; too skinny, a speed freak) and looks clean. She goes to him.

"Heading east?" Margot says, approaching slowly. She is trying to remain calm, to make eye contact, but not too much.

The man looks up at her and then around them, thinks for a moment, and sighs with resignation. "Where you going?"

"Atlanta," Margot says, the plan having solidified at some point in the night.

"I'm only going as far as Montgomery. I can take you there." Margot realizes that he looks a bit like Paul, the same dusty brown hair and hazel eyes. She smiles and then he yawns and says, "Yeah, alright, give me twenty minutes to get some breakfast in me. If you're here, you're here."

Margot knows that she will forget this man eventually, probably soon. Tucker will slip from her memory, too, deteriorating into a hazy form behind her, nothing more. If she should cross paths with him again, she will smile and nod and wait for the discomfort to build enough that he'll let her pass by with nothing more than a wish for a little good luck, maybe a teasing insult. That her mind will lose Edie, though, saddens her terribly.

Margot wanders to the ragged fenceline. The ground outside the fence is strewn with crabapples and she bends slowly to pick up as many as her hands can hold. The fruits are hard and cold and wet. She bites into one, then spits the tart meat onto the ground. In the pasture, three horses graze on the wet grass. Margot clucks her tongue and one of them looks up at her. She whistles softly. *Wthee wthee, wthee wthee.* She hitches her arms over the fence and holds the apples out and the dun stallion ambles unhurriedly toward her, an easy loping gait. The sun, creeping up over those eastern hills, begins to clear away the morning fog. The horse comes to Margot and chomps the crabapples from her outstretched hand. "Hey," she says quietly. The horse angles his head over the fence and nudges Margot in the shoulder. She can see the world reflected in the wet glass of his eyes. She gets three more crabapples from the ground and he takes them quickly. She rubs the horse's neck, his jaw. He exhales into her face.

"Hey, Boo," she says, laying her cheek against his cool, satiny muzzle. "Hi, Boo."

Acknowledgments

Thanks are owed to David Daley for all the work put into the creation of this book, and to Maya Sariahmed for her lovely design work. Thanks to the editors who previously published these stories: Andrea Drygas & Jim Shepard at *Ploughshares*; Ben George and Nick Roberts at *Ecotone*; Alex Streiff at *The Journal*; Conor Broughan at *Sycamore Review*; Robert Fogarty and Muriel Keyes at *Antioch Review*; Rebecca Morgan Frank and Barrett Bowlin at *Memorious*; Nicola Mason & Michael Griffith at *Cincinnati Review*; and Jason Lee Brown, John McNally & Rosellen Brown at *New Stories from the Midwest*.

I owe an unpayable debt of gratitude to the good people at the Iowa Writers' Workshop, including James Alan McPherson, Ethan Canin, Jennifer Vanderbes, Adam Haslett, Connie Brothers, Deb West, Jan Zenisek, and the late Frank Conroy. This book would not exist without the help and guidance of the folks at the University of Houston, including J. Kastely, Antonya Nelson, Robert Boswell, Alexander Parsons, Chitra Divakaruni, William Monroe, and Dorothy Baker, as well as my wonderful friends and colleagues at *Gulf Coast*. Thanks also to Rich Levy, Marilyn Jones, and everyone at Inprint for their extraordinary work and generosity.

I am indebted to family, friends, and colleagues for various forms of essential support and inspiration. Thanks to Travis Stansel, Kelly Lando, Nick Zivic, Robert Stansel & Tammy Marek, Bob & Jenny Strickley, David Philip Mullins, Steve Kistulentz, Thisbe Nissen, Megan Mayhew Bergman, Bret Anthony Johnston, David Lombardi, Zack Bean, and Roderic Crooks. Special thanks to my mother, Catherine O'Connell.

Unending love and gratitude to Sarah Strickley, my best reader and best friend, without whom...